THE
SWORD
OF THE
SPIRITS

Also by John Christopher
From Aladdin

THE TRIPODS SERIES
The White Mountains
The City of Gold and Lead
The Pool of Fire
When the Tripods Came

The Lotus Caves
A Dusk of Demons
The Guardians

THE SWORD OF THE SPIRITS TRILOGY
The Prince in Waiting
Beyond the Burning Lands

THE **SWORD OF THE SPIRITS** TRILOGY

THE SWORD OF THE SPIRITS

JOHN CHRISTOPHER

Aladdin

NEW YORK   LONDON   TORONTO   SYDNEY   NEW DELHI

ALADDIN

An imprint of Simon & Schuster Children's Publishing Division
1230 Avenue of the Americas, New York, NY 10020
This Aladdin paperback edition February 2015
Text copyright © 1972 by John Christopher
Cover illustration copyright © 2015 by Anton Petrov
Also available in an Aladdin hardcover edition.
All rights reserved, including the right of reproduction in whole or in part in any form.
ALADDIN is a trademark of Simon & Schuster, Inc.,
and related logo is a registered trademark of Simon & Schuster, Inc.
For information about special discounts for bulk purchases, please contact
Simon & Schuster Special Sales at 1-866-506-1949 or business@simonandschuster.com.
The Simon & Schuster Speakers Bureau can bring authors to your live event. For more
information or to book an event contact the Simon & Schuster Speakers Bureau
at 1-866-248-3049 or visit our website at www.simonspeakers.com.
Cover designed by Karin Paprocki
Interior designed by Hilary Zarycky
The text of this book was set in Venetian 301.
Manufactured in the United States of America 0115 OFF
2 4 6 8 10 9 7 5 3 1
Library of Congress Control Number 2014953411
ISBN 978-1-4814-1998-7 (hc)
ISBN 978-1-4814-1997-0 (pbk)
ISBN 978-1-4814-1999-4 (eBook)

With love to Sheila and Jenny

CONTENTS

THE
SWORD
OF THE
SPIRITS

ONE

A TRAITOR DIES

LESS THAN A WEEK AFTER I WAS ACCLAIMED Prince of Winchester the pigeons brought a message of defiance from Petersfield.

That city had been taken by my father, Prince Robert. On the advice of the Seers he had kept it, rather than exact ransom as was the custom. He had made one of the Petersfield Captains his lieutenant, but the blue and gold flag of Winchester flew from its citadel.

When my father was killed by treachery and my brother Peter reigned, the men of Petersfield accepted him in turn. He was renowned as a warrior, and had killed the man who killed my father. He ruled both cities, and if there were any in Petersfield who objected they did not do so openly but only murmured in corners.

Then my brother's Lady died, accidentally as it appeared. But when I returned from my journey beyond the Burning Lands to the city of the Wilsh, I found myself accused of her murder. In fact Ezzard the Seer had killed her, by means of the forbidden ancient power called electricity. It was done for my benefit—she was carrying the child who would bar me from succession—but I knew nothing of it.

Nevertheless my brother accused me, along with the Seer and his Acolytes. He ordered me to be burned alongside them in the palace yard. It was then that I challenged him and he accepted the challenge. We fought and his sword broke against mine—that which was forged for me by the Seers in Sanctuary. He flung himself against me, his weapon broken to a stub, and my sword took his life.

So at last I became Prince, as the Spirits had prophesied years before at the Seance of the Crowns. The crowd which had vilified me and shouted for my death cheered me instead. But that was in Winchester.

In Petersfield there were other thoughts. I had won some reputation in the north but the news was not yet widespread. They saw me as little more than a boy, a Prince by accident. They thought the time was ripe to regain their freedom.

The message that came was brief and insulting. Michael, Prince of Petersfield, sent greetings to the Prince of Winchester. He would do him no hurt so long as he stayed behind his own walls. And he was sending a gift to help him while away the time there. He was also returning something which had been loaned by his predecessor, for which Petersfield had no further use.

The gift was not long delayed. I was called to the North Gate next morning. During the night the guard had heard the sound of horsemen, but on being challenged they had turned away. They had left some things outside the gate. A wooden sword and shield such as boys use when they play at warriors, and one of those wooden horses that children put between their legs and run with, pretending they are horsemen. There was also the body of Captain Markham, my brother's lieutenant.

A crowd had gathered. They stood in silence. They

were looking at the toys and the dead man. They were also looking at me. I saw Blaine and Harding, who had bowed the knee to my father and my brother but been their enemies nevertheless. They had pledged allegiance to me, too, but with the same lying tongues. They would pull me down if they could.

Greene was there as well. He was the Captain who had commanded the expedition to the north. I spoke to him, but loud enough for others to hear.

"Have this body taken up. Tell the Seer he will be buried with full honors in the Captains' graveyard."

Greene nodded. "I will see to it, sire."

"Take up those other things also. Keep them carefully."

He was silent. They were all watching me. I paused before I went on:

"We will tie them round Michael's neck before we hang him."

They cheered at that. Greene's face spread into a grin. His fingers rolled the waxed ends of his mustache. As I had learned on the expedition he lacked inner certainty, but he obeyed orders and fought well and bravely. I said:

"How long will it take for the army to be ready?"

He said confidently: "They can be ready in three days."

"No." I shook my head; their eyes were on me. "You can do better than that. We ride north tomorrow."

There was another loud cheer, echoing back from the city's walls. I turned and left them.

I talked to Edmund in the little parlor behind the Hall of Mirrors. I sat in my father's old wooden chair, with Margry's painting of my mother hanging on the wall opposite. The morning had been gray, but with mists that were rising now. At times the sun lanced through. It would be hot in the afternoon.

Edmund was my friend, although my father had killed his and taken the crown. He had ridden with me on the expedition; and when my first sword broke in the fight with Peter it was he who had thrown me the Sword of the Spirits so that I could fight on. That sword lay now on a table by the window, unsheathed. Briefly the sun dazzled from the steel.

Edmund said: "It shines brightly."

"Rudi has been putting a polish on it. Hans brought it back to me just now."

Rudi was Master Armorer to the city. He was also a dwarf: armory was one of the trades the dwarfs kept, as an honor as well as a duty. Hans, his son, had traveled with us beyond the Burning Lands.

"A polish," Edmund said, "but not an edge. Even Rudi could not improve on the edge it has."

"No."

The sword was said to have been forged not by men but by the Spirits. I did not want to talk of this to Edmund because even to him I could not tell the truth: I had given an oath of secrecy to the Seers. To change the subject, I said:

"Rudi has been busy with a new sword for Hans. He is determined his son will go into battle as well equipped as any warrior of Winchester, and better than most."

Edmund's hand had been on the sword hilt, caressing it. He turned and said:

"Into battle? You are not letting him ride with the army?"

"Yes. He will ride beside me."

"But it is impossible," Edmund said. "A dwarf may not be a warrior."

"He rode with us to the north."

"As your servant."

"And saved my life when I was a prisoner of the Sky People."

"It was well done," Edmund said, "and you are right to reward him. But not in such a way as this."

"In what way, then?"

"With gold. No dwarf can ever have enough of that."

"This one can. Gold means nothing to him. He wants only one thing: to be a warrior. And he has earned it."

"The Captains will not be pleased."

"They will have to learn to be. Or at any rate put up with it. In the same way that Greene learned to eat the flesh of polybeasts even though at first it revolted him. In the same way that he learned to accept a polymuf as his equal at the court of King Cymru."

"But we are back in a civilized country, Luke! All that was on the other side of the Burning Lands. We have our customs and they must be kept."

I knew the customs as well as he did. Since the Disaster, when the earth had buckled and belched fire, strange things had happened. Beasts had been born misshapen, and men also. Apart from those of human stock there were dwarfs, who were a true breed, and polymufs, who might have any deformity or crookedness.

Wherever polybeasts were found they were slaughtered, and buried or burned. In the case of children the Seers examined them and made pronouncement, calling them either true man or dwarf or polymuf. Their lives must then be lived in accordance with that decree.

Polymufs were servants always, and could hold no property. They were pitied at best, more usually despised. Dwarfs, on the other hand, worked as craftsmen and were respected as such. They had goods, even land, and polymufs to serve them. The Master Armorer sat at the Prince's table in ceremonial banquets. All this was according to custom; and custom held also that only a true man could be a warrior.

I said: "I promised it to him. I will not begin my reign by breaking a promise."

"At least put it off for now. Do not take him on this campaign. Wait until things are more settled."

He meant: wait until your position is more secure. I had won my title lawfully and the crowd had cheered me for it. But the crowd was fickle, and not all my Captains were to be trusted. And I was young and inexperienced. I could not afford to make mistakes which in an older man would have been forgiven or overlooked.

I knew all this and understood that he spoke as he did for my good. I looked at him with fondness. He was taller than I and far more handsome; but the long face was frowning, the blue eyes worried. I put my arm on his shoulder.

"Do not fret. They will do as I say as long as I give them a victory over Petersfield. And if I fail they will pull me down whether or not a dwarf rides with the army."

Later that day I saw the new Seer, the one who had been sent to replace Ezzard. His name was Grimm, but it belied him. He was a large and portly man, amply filling his Seer's black coat. He was taciturn in public, as a Seer must be; when he spoke his voice was not harsh like Ezzard's but calm and easy.

I did not see him at the Seer's House but at the palace. By having Ezzard executed I had freed myself of suspicion of complicity in his crime, and the High Seers had confirmed this when they condemned him as one driven mad by false Spirits. But they had agreed that it would be wise for me to seem to stay aloof from the new Seer, at least for the time being. He might come to the palace but I would not go to him, except to a Seance in the way of duty and observance.

Like Edmund, Grimm was unhappy, though not about Hans. He knew nothing of that. It was the campaign that troubled him. He said:

"Luke, it is folly to risk everything at this stage. You need time to consolidate. Things have happened so fast. There should be a breathing space."

I said: "Tell that to Michael of Petersfield. Or to the spirit of Markham, whom we buried this morning."

"He has baited you and you have risen to the bait. It is what he wanted."

I shrugged. "Maybe so. It makes no difference. I could do nothing else."

"You could have laughed it off: the joke was feeble enough."

"And the dead man? Does one laugh off a corpse also?"

"He was not of this city. They could not say his spirit called on you."

"Not of this city, but he served it. He was lieutenant to my father, to my brother, and for a few short days to me. My honor requires me to avenge him."

Grimm scratched his broad white skull, his head being shaven as befitted his office. He said:

"This business of honor wearies me. I hope you are not going to take it too seriously, Luke."

I was aware yet again of the division in my nature and my mind. I knew and understood what Grimm meant. To him and the other Seers such things as honor and glory were of no importance in themselves: they only mattered insofar as they served that larger plan to which their lives were devoted.

The plan was for the renewal of that part of human knowledge which had been abandoned since the Disaster. Those who survived the heaving and twisting of the earth had blamed Science for their miseries. The blame was wrongly placed because the cataclysm had been one of nature, not of man, but the belief was firmly held. In the days after the cities crumbled and crashed, people turned against machines and tore to pieces any who made or used them.

They turned also to a worship of Spirits. These were said to be of two kinds: the Spirits of the dead, and those other Spirits who had never lived in the flesh but who invisibly plagued or benefited men's lives, and served the Great Spirit who ruled and had made everything. In Seances the Spirits talked to the worshipers in darkened rooms, and the Seers presented and interpreted them.

So it was believed. In fact the Seers created the voices, and even the appearances of Spirits, by trickery and the use of those very machines which they claimed to condemn. Their purpose was to gain control of all the civilized lands. When their control was complete they thought they could wean men from superstition and back to science.

But in the civilized lands cities warred against each other, under many different Princes. The first aim of the Seers must be to unite the cities under one ruler. This was the task I had been chosen to undertake. Because of it my father had been made ruler, and after his death I had been smuggled from the city to the safety of Sanctuary where the High Seers lived. Because of it, though without my knowledge or even the knowledge of the High Seers, Ezzard had murdered my brother's wife.

Thus the Seers had gained their first objective. I was Prince of Winchester, a city strong in itself and well placed to conquer others. All this I knew and had accepted and was pledged to serve. But I was moved by other things as well.

I had been reared as a warrior, son of a man who had risen from the ranks and gained nobility on the field of battle. Honor was no empty term to me; nor did it weary me. It was something which had touched my life as long as I could remember. It might mean nothing to the Seers, who spent so much time in trickery and deceit—albeit to a worthy end. But I knew I could not live their way.

I said to Grimm: "Look on it like this. You want me to rule all the cities of the south, in your behalf. My father took Petersfield. Will it do to let that city slip from our grasp?"

"We will get Petersfield back for you," Grimm said. "Only give us time. Trevelyan will see to it." Trevelyan was Seer of Petersfield. "In the short term Michael may hold the city and defy you. But in the long term we shall have him. We opened Petersfield's walls to your father, and we can do it again."

"And will Blaine and Harding sit quietly here in Winchester while you go about your plottings? They accept me as Prince, but the moment I show myself to be weak or cowardly I will have them at my throat. Have sense."

He was only half persuaded. He said: "We could handle Blaine and Harding."

"So can I," I said. "In my own way."

We rode out next morning into a white mist. One could see no farther than a few yards in any direction. Our progress had to be slow, with our outriders keeping close. We followed the river road to the west, skirting the Downs. It was the longer way, but easier.

Weather had changed greatly since the Disaster. Our seasons were colder than they had been in ancient times, our skies cloudier. This was partly due to the ash flung into the sky from the Burning Lands. There was much rain and periods of settled weather were rare. And when the sun might otherwise have shone, it was as likely that mists would rise from the earth and block its heat.

This happened now. The previous day the sun had burned a path through for a few hours but today the mists were too strong for it. We saw no more than a pale disk at midday. By the time we made camp in the evening the mists were thicker than ever, clammily cold and gray.

Making camp was not easy. Men stumbled over each other and cursed each other's carelessness. And the baggage train, having been hastily put together, lacked certain things. We were reckoning to get our meat from Petersfield farms but we had found no cattle yet. Rations were short: dried beef and bread only.

This and the clinging chill of the mist discouraged the men. I made a round of the camp and found them taciturn and sullen. I tried to cheer them but with poor success. I was not skilled in wooing my fellows and never had been. Their sullenness kindled a similar feeling in my own mind. I tried to master it, and smile and chaff them. But the words and smiles seemed false even to me.

Among Harding's tents I asked if there was anything that was needed. It was a routine question, not expected to be answered, and elsewhere it had not been. But here a man, disguised by the mist, answered roughly:

"If you cannot give us decent food, at least give us Prince's weather."

I did not know how to answer. For that matter I could not tell who had spoken. There was a grumbling murmur from other throats. Then Harding spoke from my side:

"Sergeant! Find that man and bring him here."

His voice was cold and sharp. He himself was a cold, sharp-featured man, slight of body but strong and wiry. He kept good order within his troop. The man was brought to us at once.

He was a man called Morgan. His frame was as large as Harding's was slight. He stood well above six feet tall. There would have been risk of his being called a polymuf giant except that his body was well proportioned. He stood with the Sergeant at his side, looking down on us both.

Harding said: "When your Prince speaks you listen. You do not answer back. I will have no such insolence in my troop. Ten lashes, Sergeant."

The Sergeant saluted. "First thing in the morning, Captain?"

"No," Harding said. "Here and now. In front of his Prince, whom he insulted. And see that they are well laid on."

Morgan stared with silent hatred, but not at Harding. His eyes were on me. I thought of asking for clemency but knew it would only make matters worse. Harding's man had spoken back and it was Harding's right to have him punished.

He was stripped above the waist and made to kneel in front of us. Another soldier stood over him and lashed him. I do not know if the strokes were well laid on, as Harding had commanded, because I did not look at his naked back. I watched his face, staring down at the earth. He took his punishment impassively but on the last few strokes could not help wincing.

Harding said: "Let no other man of this troop shame himself and it by failing to pay due respect to his Prince. It will be fifty lashes next time."

I looked at Morgan's back when they gave him his shirt again. The lash had not broken the skin but there were dark red weals in neat rows. He did not put the shirt on—he would need ointment from the surgeon first—but saluted and walked away.

His eyes looked into mine again before he was lost in the mist. It was Harding who had ordered the lashing, but I who had gained an enemy. Harding came well out of this, I saw. In maintaining his own authority he had filched from mine. They would see me as a boy, Harding as my protector who might, at the right moment, supplant a weakling.

The mist was a little less thick next day and we made more progress. We were in Petersfield lands and for that reason must go warily. Grimm had told me before we set out that the Petersfield army had not left the city—he had the news from their Seer by radio—but they might have done so since. I told Greene to post a double line of scouts.

We came within sight of the city in late afternoon. We showed ourselves but did not approach the walls closely. We retreated into the mist, which was thickening again, and made camp on high ground to the north.

The men were in better heart. We had found cattle which we killed and roasted. We had also found a country alehouse, and the men washed their victuals down with Petersfield ale. They claimed it was poor thin stuff compared with our own, but I warned Greene all the same that the Sergeants must make sure they did not drink too freely. I did not want an army with sore heads if the Petersfield warriors came out next day.

They did not come out, though. The weather had changed. The mist had gone and a fresh wind blew from the north. The sky was cloudy but visibility was good. We made a circuit of their walls. A few arrows hissed through the air at us, falling short. Nothing else happened.

I sent a herald to them in the afternoon. This was according to custom where an army was not already in the field. My message was to Captain Michael Smith. The Prince of Winchester sent him greeting. If he surrendered himself and opened the gates of the city to its rightful Prince, he would have fair trial by the Captains for his murder of the Prince's lieutenant. If not, the swords of Winchester were ready to cut him down, along with any other rebels rash enough to follow him.

The herald was that Captain Barnes who had arrested me at my brother's command on my return from beyond the Burning Lands. He was a tall, thin, gray-haired man, sparing of speech but full of loyalty. He had served my brother and now served me. I could trust him as I could not trust all my Captains.

Returning, he dismounted and his horse was led away, the white cloth of truce blowing from the saddle. I said:

"Well, John?"

The other Captains were present. Barnes said awkwardly:

"I was given a message, sire."

"Tell it, then."

I could have taken him off and got the message in private; but I would not do that. It was plainly an insult. I would receive it publicly.

Barnes said woodenly: "This is the message I was given, sire. 'The Prince of Petersfield bids little Luke go home and play with the toys he sent him. He does not go into battle against children, or those who follow a child.'"

My Captains watched me, from Wilson the eldest

to Edmund, little older than myself. Blaine watched from his fat face and Harding from his meager one. Greene put up a hand to twirl his mustache.

I said: "I have heard. Thank you for your office."

I talked to Edmund later. He said:

"He shows himself inferior by refusing your challenge. Everyone must see that."

"Must they? And how will the talk run in the alehouses if we go back to Winchester with our swords still sheathed? That the men of Petersfield mocked them for letting themselves be ruled by a boy. That they judged us unworthy of battle."

"No one of sense will say such a thing."

"I spoke of men in alehouses, not men of sense. And do men of sense sway a mob? They were not men of sense who shouted for my death a week ago."

"You have no choice, Luke, anyway. They will not come out and you cannot make them. Nor can you storm the city. Your father did, but only because they were fool enough to use a machine, which the Spirits caused to blow up and breach the wall. It has been strongly rebuilt and we should have small hope of scaling it."

"He will come out," I said. "I will bring him out."

Edmund shook his head. "How?"

I told him. He listened in disbelief. "You cannot do it."

"You will see what I can do."

I stood with the Captains on a knoll. A little below us and half a mile away were the walls of Petersfield. There was open ground between: grazing meadows and wheatfields. The wheat moved in the wind. I said to Greene:

"Send a squad of men with torches to fire the wheat."

Greene stared, too staggered for speech. It was Blaine who spoke.

"You cannot do such a thing! It is against all custom."

Wheat meant bread for the long hard winter. It stood for life itself. No one rode or fought over growing wheat, and if a campaign ever lasted through summer, harvesting put an end to it.

I said to Greene: "You heard me. That field below us first."

If Greene had hesitated further, the others might have got together and stopped me. As it was they the soldiers, but said when we were left alone:

"Well, Luke, I hope they did not give you too hard a time of it."

I stared at him. I was covered with filth and my head throbbed. The cut beneath my eye was swelling. I said:

"Hard enough, sir. It is kind of you to inquire."

"Listen," he said, "you did a foolish thing in going out last night. You were caught, and punishment followed. It is something that must be accepted."

"I was brought to you. You did not need to hand me back to them, to ask to have me put in the stocks."

"No? I think we did. You are by your age plainly a trainee, too young to have taken vows and so lacking the protection of our cloth. It is essential for the common people to respect that cloth. Since you disgraced it in their eyes, it was necessary that those eyes should witness your thing. To be made sport of by the mob is another."

I said: "There are things due to me also. My father was Prince of a greater city than this. Punishment is one thing. To be made sport of by the mob is another."

"It offends your dignity?"

"I have been trained to fight," I said, "to face wounding or death, even death by execution. But not to endure the mockery of curs. I saw polymufs grinning at me."

"Your dignity is not important. That is something you have to learn."

"But the dignity of the High Seers is?"

Murphy shook his head. "No. What is important is the restoration of human order and human knowledge. Everything must serve that."

I looked at him angrily, in silence. He said:

"Remember that we made your father Prince and made you Prince in Waiting. We brought you from Winchester when there was a score of men eager to cut you down, confident that the new Prince, your brother, would thank them for it, and glad anyway to see one Perry the less. We have kept you in the Sanctuary and may yet restore you to this dignity which you prize so much."

"Yet! In what time? Five years? Ten? Fifty, perhaps?"

"Sooner, I hope." He relaxed and smiled. "How

would you like to leave the Sanctuary and go back to Winchester, Luke?"

I shook my head. "Do not mock me, sir."

"No mocking. I have a Christmas gift for you. Your brother seeks your return and pledges his word to your safety."

I said, scarcely trusting myself to believe it: "This is not a joke?"

"News came this morning while you were in the stocks. Your brother is married to a Christian, as you know. The man they say was a god was born, they also say, on this day more than twenty-two centuries ago. Perhaps she asked it of your brother; the Christians' ways are strange."

I thought of the Christians putting themselves between me and the mob. I wondered if they were still in the stocks, and still chanting.

I said: "It is really true? When do I leave?"

"You are eager to be rid of us," Murphy said. "We return to the Sanctuary tomorrow and you will leave a few days after that."

I believed it now and forgot my anger and my bruises. I forgot even the filth with which I was smeared. It was Murphy who reminded me of it. Sniffing, he said:

"A more urgent need is that you have a bath and change into clean linen. Our somber black for a while still. But because of your disgrace you will not appear at any ceremonies, nor sit solemn at the banquet. That is another good thing you get from today's misfortunes."

TWO

TOASTS AT A BANQUET

EZZARD ACCOMPANIED ME ON MY RETURN to Winchester. It was accepted by Peter that my life had been in danger in the days following our father's murder and his own accession, and that the Seer had been right to take me away. That was the official story, but I imagined there was more to it. Though he had married a Christian Peter himself was a Spiritist, as far as he was anything, and so also were his Captains. It was not easy even for a strong Prince to defy the Seers for long.

We went on horseback, openly, Ezzard in Seer's robes and I in clothes befitting my rank. I wore also a sword, a parting gift from the High Seers: the Sword of the Spirits which had been promised to me when they came to Winchester after the taking of Petersfield. Handing it to me, Murphy said:

"Steel, case-hardened in an induction furnace. You will find no metal to come near it, and no blade that will match it in strength and cutting edge. Look after it and it will serve you well."

We called at various towns on our way. Everywhere Ezzard let it be known that I was returning on my brother's invitation, thus binding his honor more firmly to my safety. The precaution, as he said, was probably unnecessary, but it was best to take no chances. So despite my impatience we did not hurry on the journey.

But at last, having spent the night as guests of its Prince, we left Andover in the morning and I had high hopes of reaching Winchester by night. The weather dashed these: a light fall of snow before midday turned, in the afternoon, into a driving blizzard. We had passed Headbourne Worthy, the nearest village north of the city, and had not much more than a mile to go. The distance was tantalizingly short but as the wind howled and the blinding snow drove into our faces, even I was forced to agree that we must seek shelter. We found it in a farm, where we were respectfully received and well looked after. They gave us tidings of the city, to which I listened greedily. The farmer and his wife had a son, a boy of twelve. He told me he had seen me win the Sword of Honor in the Contest, and recited a full account of it. His dream was to be a warrior, and I told him to come to me when he was of age and I would enlist him in my troop. He was deeply grateful for the promise, which I thought was likely to profit me also. He was a strong, capable lad, with the makings of a soldier. His mother was less pleased, since he was her only son, but she would reconcile herself to losing him: she must have known he was not the sort of boy to stay on a farm once he was grown.

I had feared, when we retired to bed with the blizzard still howling, that we might be immured in the farmhouse for days. The morning dawned clear, however, the sky gray but no longer threatening, and when the servants had cut a path through drifted snow to the stable we were able to leave. Our horses floundered at times where the snow was loosely packed but we made fair progress. I saw, even in this landscape blanketed in white, landmarks I knew: Wherry's mill, a clump of fir trees that leaned in toward each other like conspirators, a rusty crumbling shaft that came from the ancient times and was shunned by children, being thought to harbor ghosts. And beyond these, so familiar and so dear, the walls of my native city. I was home again. Turning my head so that Ezzard would not see, I put up my sleeve and brushed the dampness from my eyes.

If I had any doubts of my welcome they were dispelled by the shout of joy from the guard on the North Gate. Its Sergeant, who had been in my father's troop when he was still a Captain and whom I could remember, when I was five or six, fencing with me with wooden sticks for swords, gave me the ceremonial salute, and his men yelled their heads off in acclamation. The ordinary people took up the cry and followed us through the streets as we rode to the palace. And the news must have gone ahead because when we reached the palace yard many of the Captains were assembled. I saw Greene and Meredith and Nicoll, small watchful Harding who had hoped to he Prince after my father's death, and blustering Blaine who had cuffed me into a corner when I urged them to ride against our own walls to avenge him. I saw Edmund's brother, Charles, whose father had been Prince until my father, with Ezzard's help, unseated him. And last I saw my brother, who held that title which the Spirits, through Ezzard's trickery, had promised to me: Prince of Winchester.

I dismounted and let a soldier take my horse. I walked toward Peter, my feet sinking into snow which the polymufs had not yet had time to clear away. I bowed my head and said:

"Greetings, sire."

He put a hand on my shoulder. He said, smiling:

"No ceremony between brothers! Come in, Luke, and we will drink your health."

The day of my return had been proclaimed a feast, and in the evening there was to be a banquet in celebration. Meanwhile there was the confusion of people greeting me. Some were sincere; others, I very well knew, were not. Blaine, who fulsomely gave thanks to the Spirits for protecting me, would have liked to slip a dagger between my ribs. Harding, a more wily man, would have preferred to watch him, or any other, do it. But there were those like Sergeant Burke, who looked after me on my first campaign, and Wilson, my father's most trusted comrade, whose gladness was real and unmistakable. There was also Ann, the Prince's Lady.

I had seen little of her in the old days. The estrangement between Peter and me had kept me from visiting the house in the River Road where they lived; and of course she was a Christian and so of no importance in the city.

I had known her as a quiet, perhaps simple woman, without beauty or indeed much else to explain my brother's choosing her. When I paid my respects I found she had only one woman in attendance—my mother had never had less than half a dozen. This one she dismissed, if dismissal is the right term to use of what was no more than a request, modestly put, that we might be left alone together. She said:

"Let me look at you. Have they been taking proper care of you, your High Seers? You are paler than you were. And taller. And they have shaved your head, but that will soon grow. We shall see that mop of fierce black hair again before spring."

I was surprised that she paid me such attention, or remembered me so well. And her smile surprised me with its warmth, and the way it changed a face which I had thought plain and insignificant. I made some sort of reply and she said:

"I cannot express how glad I am to see you, Luke. Not only for your sake but for Peter's. He could not be happy, knowing you were in exile and from fear of him. He would never have harmed you, and this reconciliation gladdens his heart. He has been so much happier since he asked the Seers to send you back and they agreed."

And also, I guessed, since he had done that which was pleasing to his wife's strange Christian conscience. Nor had I any doubt that the main urging for my recall had come from her. Her influence over him was plainly great and this was something to be remembered. I could not see why it should be so— why a man should let any woman dominate his mind—but the fact that one did not understand a thing was no reason for not weighing its effects. There would not be many things in which Peter would run counter to her wishes.

I said: "I am glad to be back, my Lady."

She shook her head. "Call me Ann, as your sister. My Lady is not a title I like, in any case. There is only one who merits it—the mother of our Lord."

The Lord being, as Murphy had explained, the Christian god. It was puzzling to think of a god with a mother but I thought it best to ask no questions. I was not, in any case, interested in the oddities of their religion. We talked together for a time and kissed as brother and sister when we parted.

I had sent messages to Edmund and Martin, saying I would be at our usual meeting place at four of the afternoon. I got to the Ruins a little before that. I went down the stairs and, lighting my way with a candle, through the secret way to the hidden door and our den behind it. Inside I found an oil lamp which I lit. It was still strange not to command the bright steady light of electricity at the flick of a switch; the illumination from the lamp was dim and patchy, leaving shadows in the corners. But even by its feeble glow I could see that the place had fallen into disuse. Dust was thick on every surface. The chessboard was set out with pieces and a spider had stretched its web across them. That probably meant that Martin had been here last. It was he who was keen on chess problems and Edmund, in any case, would have tidied up before leaving: he could not bear disorder.

I heard footsteps. The door was pushed open and Edmund came in. He said:

"You are here before me, Luke."

We looked at each other for a moment before I put out my hand and he took it in a firm grip. I remembered that he had offered to go with me into exile, and that when I escaped instead with Ezzard I had sent him no word. But the constraint between us came from my side, not his. I had looked forward so much to seeing him but did not know what to say. I said awkwardly:

"You do not come here now?"

"Not since you left." He looked round the room. "Nor Martin, either, it would seem."

"You have not been seeing Martin?"

He shrugged. "Now and then, by chance. He is busy with his studies and I have had my own concerns."

We talked, but the awkwardness remained. I

think we were both glad to hear Martin approaching. He came to me and shook hands also. Edmund began to shake with laughter. I asked him:

"What is it? A good joke?"

It took him a moment to control himself sufficiently to speak. He said, gasping:

"It was the sight of the pair of you—those two shaved heads . . ."

Martin stared at him owlishly: he had taken to wearing spectacles since I last saw him and the effect, together with the long black robe of an Acolyte, was slightly comic. I realized I must look nearly as odd, if not odder, in warrior's leather but with a naked skull, and laughed as well. Martin joined in. We stood there, the small chamber echoing with our laughter, and the feeling of strangeness and uncertainty dissolved in it.

"Thank the Great yours is only temporary," Edmund said to me, still laughing. "I would have felt truly forsaken had you both turned Acolyte. And one could not rule out the possibility, Luke, since you were living in the Sanctuary with the High Seers. They might well have talked you into it!"

"It would need a great deal of talking," I said.

"And there is such a thing as aptitude. I do not think the High Seers ever fancied me as a recruit to the Order."

"They cropped your head."

"There was a reason for that."

I was on the point of saying that they had cropped their own as well before I remembered to guard my tongue. Edmund, flinging himself onto one of the chairs and sitting backward astride it, said:

"But what is it like there? Is it true that you get to the Sanctuary by climbing up a rainbow? And that you eat clouds and drink butterfly milk? What have you been doing all the time you have been away?"

Martin said quickly: "He cannot tell us about it. It is forbidden for him to tell or for us to listen."

In this same place Edmund had asked Martin, newly made an Acolyte, about the secrets he had learned and I, on his behalf, had said much the same as he was saying now. I had not guessed what secrets there might be, nor how soon I would be made privy to them. I wondered how much Martin himself knew; even with him I dared not speak freely of what I had seen.

I said: "It is all dull stuff, anyway. Tell me what

has been happening here in Winchester since I've been gone."

They told me the news: how such a one had broken a leg in a fall out hunting, how another had perpetrated an elaborate jest against Blaine's son Henry and got into trouble when Blaine himself was tricked by it, how one of the Dwarf Coiners of the Prince's Mint had been found to have debased the gold but had fled before he could be punished. Who had been promoted, who fallen from favor. Who won the toboggan race which was held yearly in the High Street after the first snow. I listened with an interest whetted by the months of confinement to the duller conversation of the High Seers. Martin said:

"But the really interesting thing happened only two days ago, when the peddler came."

"The peddler?" I asked.

Edmund said: "He has goods to sell, but you could as well call him liar as peddler. He says he has come across the Burning Lands, from some city far to the north."

I nodded. "I have heard tell of him. You think he lies?"

"What else? No man can cross the Burning Lands. Peddlers always have tall tales. They are for the women, to catch their interest so that afterward they can sell them trinkets at fancy prices. It is just that this one has a taller tale than most."

"He wears strange clothes," Martin said.

"Which he claims is the garb of his native land. I could devise something of the sort myself. With a pouch just above the waist, perhaps, for keeping rain off my head when I was carrying it under my arm!"

The men with their heads beneath their arms who would come from beyond the Burning Lands was one of the fantasies with which polymuf maids sometimes frightened naughty children. Edmund and I laughed, but Martin said:

"It is not only his clothes that are different. The things he sells are, also. I looked at a necklace which my cousin bought. The workmanship was not like any I have seen."

"There are always new fashions in necklaces," Edmund said. "It means nothing."

"But if the fires of the Burning Lands *are* dying down, and one could cross them . . ."

"One would find savages and polybeasts. What else?"

"Perhaps another city, as he says."

"In any case, who cares?" Edmund said. "There is enough to concern us in this city." He turned to me, dismissing the other topic. "Luke, I am glad to see you again. But are you safe?"

"I think so. And the High Seers would not have sent me here unless they thought the same."

"The Spirits named you, not Peter, Prince in Waiting. And promised you glory. This is something that will be remembered, and for some the memory of it will be a stink in their nostrils."

"I trust my brother. And his honor is pledged."

And his will, I thought, under the bidding of his Lady's conscience; but I did not say that. Edmund said:

"Do you know the story of Donald the Red?"

"No."

"I had it from a polymuf maid, an old woman who had been in the palace in my grandfather's day." At a time, I did not need reminding, when my grandfather was a humble carpenter with a strong son eager to exchange the adz for the sword. "He was a

Captain who fought well in the campaigns and was popular with the other Captains. For two years, while our army did badly he himself scored great successes. There was talk of a plot to make him Prince, and other talk of accusing him of treason before the plot could succeed. My grandfather would have none of that, despite the urgings of his friends. But in the next campaign Red Donald was killed and it was said his wound was in the back. It was not my grandfather's doing, but the man died. Your brother might have friends of a similar mind."

This was true, and true that Ann's Christian conscience could not hold her husband guilty of a murder planned by others, a deed of which he knew nothing. I was, of course, under the special protection of the Seers; but so had my father been and it had not saved him. I said, smiling:

"Thank you for the warning! But I do not think I am in any danger."

"All the same," Edmund said, "if I were you I should keep my back well guarded."

The banquet was held in the Great Hall. I sat at the right hand of the Prince and as guest of honor drank with him from the great gold pot which had been our father's, and Prince Stephen's and Prince Egbert's before that. No women were present, of course. The Captains sat above the first salt, other dignitaries between the first and second, and lesser guests below. I saw my old friend, Rudi the Armorer Dwarf, and catching my eye from that distance he raised his pot to me in greeting.

After the last of the meats were cleared and before the sweets were brought it fell to me to give the Prince's toast. I stood and the company with me. I lifted the golden pot and gave the health of the Prince of Winchester. The cry echoed down the table, and we drank.

My brother rose as I took my seat. He said:

"I would have you drink again. This time to Luke, my brother."

Afterward he remained standing. He said:

"And I have news for you and him. Tonight I make him Captain." His raised hand quelled the murmur of surprise and applause. "He is young for the rank but already capable, and promises better. And there is something else that I would say."

I looked at him standing by me. Although I was

still growing I knew I would never match his height, which was two inches over six feet. He had my father's fair hair and breadth of face and chest. The brooding expression which once had marred his features had gone, replaced by an easy smiling confidence. He was a true Prince. I wished I could feel more glad of that.

"You do not need reminding," he went on, "of certain things that have been between us, and I do not wish to dwell on them. But one is better spoken of than left hidden. There was a Seance, after my father's acclamation as Prince, in which this brother of mine was named Prince in Waiting and promised a great and glorious future. Yet I am Prince of Winchester, though named by no Spirit, and he is not."

He paused and they were silent, waiting on his words. My brother looked down at Ezzard, who sat next to him on the other side.

"As the Seer himself will tell you, the prophecies of the Spirits are not always what they seem. Luke may still have a destiny of triumph, in another city, perhaps even another land. In this city I rule, and will do so. But I say this to you: after my Lady, my brother is the most precious to me of all. I pledge myself, by my honor as Prince, by the Great Spirit, and by any other god that may be, to protect and care for him. I say this also: if harm should come to him I will hunt down the man who does it and kill him with my own hands."

There was a moment's silence before they started cheering and banging their pots. He stood there smiling. When at last the noise died down, he said:

"There will be no dissension between us brothers. By his return Luke declares this also, and renounces the claims that others made for him. So I ask him now to seal the contract as I have done. I ask him, by the Great Spirit, to pledge allegiance to me and to my heirs."

I fought to control my face against the feelings that pressed in on me. Apart from anything else I was astounded: I would not have thought he had such guile. Had the Christian priest, perhaps, counseled him? Or Ann? I could not believe it of her. I wondered what Ezzard was thinking; whatever it was he would show nothing. I forced a smile to my lips and kept it there as I rose to face the two long lines of faces. In the strongest voice I could muster, I said:

"In the name of the Great Spirit, I pledge my allegiance to Peter, Prince of Winchester, and to his heirs."

They cheered at that, though I thought the face of Blaine, who sat a little way down the table, showed puzzlement: his eyes in their folds of fat were narrowed. Harding, sitting opposite, was impassive as always.

My brother put his hand on my shoulder. I felt its weight as strong, oppressive, and would have liked to shake it off. He said:

"There will be no more talk of dispute between us. Luke stands at my right hand and will always do so. The city is well guarded. If I should die in next summer's battles, or any summer after that, Luke will see to things until a son of mine is old enough to wear a sword."

There was something strange; not in his words but in the manner of speaking them. It was proper for a warrior to face death with a light heart, but the exultation in his voice meant more than that. Others, too, had sensed it. I saw Blaine lean forward, watching, hand tugging at his beard.

My brother said: "So one more thing: one more

toast to drink! And for this we will all stand because we toast one who is not here—not in this room and not yet in this world."

He lifted the golden pot that stood between us.

"My Lady is with child. Drink to my son to be— your future Prince!"

THREE

THE PRINCE'S LADY

NEXT MORNING I SAT WITH EZZARD IN HIS parlor. Not many people were received there but it was still furnished with the trappings of a Seer. Chairs, stools and table, sideboard and bookcase were of dark fumed oak, and the long curtains at the windows were black velvet. From facing walls a stuffed owl, wings lifted, stared with small glass eyes of frozen fury at a stuffed eagle. There were three skulls on the sideboard and a Book of the Spirits thickly bound in white calf. In the center of the table stood the sphere of milky crystal on an ebony base which Ezzard was thought to use in receiving messages from the Spirits, and from the High Seers in the Sanctuary.

The radio transmitter and receiver, through which the messages in fact were passed, was in a small room above this. Ezzard showed me the panel in the wall which, pressed at a certain point, opened a way to the stairs that led to it. I asked him:

"And such things are in all the Seers' Houses? But how can you trust the workmen not to talk?"

"When a Seer's House is built," Ezzard said, "some things are done by the dwarfs, but not all. That which is sacred to the Spirits is left to the Seer and his Acolytes, and the dwarfs accept this. To serve this Order, Luke, requires more than an ability to read books and wear a solemn face and seem to pray: much more. Even the solemnity and the praying are probably less easy than you think, but there are also skills to learn and hard labor in applying them."

I nodded. "I see that."

He smiled. "You would never have made an Acolyte, but that is not your part in our business."

"Do I still have a part? After last night surely your plans for me are finished."

"Because a woman is with child? It will not even be born till summer."

"Already it makes the future."

"And may be a girl."

"The odds are against it. My father's family ran to sons, and my brother's wife was a girl with four brothers, with uncles but no aunts. And even if this one should be a girl there will be others. They will have sons, and I am pledged to aid and serve them."

"A forced oath," Ezzard said, "is not binding. It happened once before in this city, in very ancient days, that a Prince was crowned in breach of such an oath, sworn on holy relics."

I shook my head. "I want no precedents for treachery. I swore the oath and will keep it. My honor requires that. There would be no joy in living if I broke it."

Ezzard stared at me a moment in silence, blue eyes cold in the craggy white face. He said:

"What joy do you think there is in my life, Luke? Do you think I delight in this blackness that surrounds me? Not just the blackness of furnishings and clothes. My whole life is a cheat, and must be. Every day must be given up to deception, to further lies. What if my honor were to make demands? The cause we serve is greater than small things like one man's honor."

I said stubbornly: "I am sorry, sir, but it is something I cannot accept. My mind is different from yours, perhaps. I will serve your ends as far as I can, but my honor comes first."

"Yes." He paused. "Yes. And you serve us best by being what you are. I know you, Luke, and know what may be asked of you. It is a great deal. But I also know what may not be asked, and will not ask it. As to present circumstances, we will not worry too much yet."

He drew breath deeply: a sigh, if one could imagine such a thing from so austere a man.

"We must all be patient. And you and I, Luke, must not see too much of each other. It is known that the Seers protected you, but as was said last night the time for that is past. Men respect the Seers, as is necessary, but are also wary of them. The smell of this black cloth must not cling to you, now that you are back in the palace and a Captain of the Prince's army. So do not come here again unless I summon you."

"I shall still see Martin. He is my friend."

"Yes. That is reasonable. But of him too you will see less. As I have said, an Acolyte has other things to do than study and pray. He will not have much time to spare for idling in that cell beneath the Ruins."

"He told you of it?"

"No," Ezzard said. "He did not need to. We have kept close watch on you, Luke. And must do so. You are the piece on which our hopes are pinned. Nothing has changed there."

The peddler was a man in his early thirties, of medium build and height. Physically there was nothing unusual to him: he had black hair and beard, keen eyes, the stance of someone who spends much time trudging poor roads. But his clothes were not such as peddlers commonly wore. They were gayer in color and unfamiliar in fashion. Beneath a red cloak, unusually short but having a part, secured with pearly buttons, that could be let down, he wore baggy trousers of a brighter green than I could recall seeing in a cloth, and leather gaiters above his boots. These last were shiny black with silver buckles at the front.

He presented himself to Peter at an assembly of the Captains. He bowed deeply, putting one hand behind him into the small of his back, a gesture so comic that many smiled, and introduced himself in a barbarous accent. His name, he said, was Yews, and he came from the city of Klan Gothlen, in the land of the Wilsh. He offered the Prince a gift for his Lady.

It was a contraption in the shape of a small broken hoop, covered with bright stones. It was to be worn across the top of the head, he explained, and demonstrated this by opening it out and ludicrously pressing it in place for a moment over his own black thatch.

My brother thanked him gravely. He asked him how he had made his way so far, through such hazards. And how had he managed to cross the Burning Lands?

There had been a party of them, the peddler explained. For a long time his people had traded into the countries of the savages. There were risks—he shrugged expressively—but there were also profits. And for years it had been known that the Burning Lands were cooling: there were fewer mountains that spurted fire and the fires themselves, with their flows of molten rock, were smaller. There was a pass and others before had ventured part way in but had been forced to turn back—as his companions this time had also done. He had pushed on, gambling that he would get through before the heat from the ground overcame him. It had been a near thing but he had succeeded.

Peter said, looking at the polish and the shining buckles: "Your boots have stood it well. You must have good leather in the land of the Wilsh."

The peddler shook his head. "I threw away the ones I wore. They were well-nigh scorched through."

"And your horse? Did you have spare hoofs for him?"

"No, sire. But I made him boots of leather; and bound them round, as I did my own, with a cloth that we have in my country. It is woven from a stone called chrysotile which protects against heat."

A cloth woven from stone? But the very improbability made his tale convincing. My brother put other questions to him, which he answered as readily. His city lay in mountainous country and lacked the richness of land we took for granted. Their sheep gave poorer wool and stringier mutton; what corn they had was scant and small-eared. But their craftsmen, he thought, made things which our people might enjoy. He would hope to return another time and bring others.

"Your story is an interesting one," Peter said. "If we send an embassy to your city, will it be received in peace?"

"How not?" the peddler said. "In peace and with rejoicing. We are a civilized people."

Peter dismissed the peddler, with a present of gold that brought a gleam to his eye. He dismissed the Captains also, but asked me to stay. We went together to the little room where my father had liked to sit, away from the noise and ceremony of the court. He sat in my father's old armchair and turned the ornament the peddler had given him in his hands.

"Copper," he said, "though more highly burnished than is common with us. And the stones are pretty but not precious. Some are glass."

I said: "One does not expect a rich gift from a peddler. You were more than generous in return."

"Cheer up, Luke! We are neither of us likely to die just yet. And it gives you the chance to think again as well. I would not hold you to your word, either."

I said, stammering: "You . . . do not need to."

"Don't I?" She looked at me, amused. "You would make a poor courtier, Luke. But being a Prince you have no need to play that role. And I am glad of it. We have glib courtiers enough in Klan Gothlen. You are a warrior. Now, tell me about all your battles and victories."

When Edmund joined us he took her hands and kissed her on the cheek as I had done. I was glad to see them so pleased to see each other. They fell to chattering at once, about people we had known at the court of King Cymru. I recalled them well enough myself, but had nothing to say of them.

She had no warning to give to him, of course, so there was no shadow of seriousness and therefore less constraint. In fact his presence made things easier for me as well. I could relax, listening to them talk. I did not have much to contribute, but it was enough to hear them.

Edmund spoke of the banquet which would cele-
brate her coming. She said eagerly that she loved
banquets; she wished it were this evening instead of
the next day. Edmund chaffed her, saying it was her
vanity that prompted the wish: to sit at the head of
the table and see the eyes of all Winchester's
Captains engrossed with her beauty.

She tossed her head. "I am not so vain as to think
your Captains must look at me in preference to your
own ladies."

"Perhaps they would not if they had a choice. But
since you will be the only lady present, at whom else
should they look? At each other?"

"The only lady present?" She looked at me.
"Surely not! Your ladies will not refuse to greet
me?"

"No," I said, "but it is not our custom to have
ladies at our banquets. That was something we
found strange in your city."

"Can you not change your custom?"

"It would not be easy."

Edmund laughed and we both looked at him. He
said:

"I was thinking of another custom that one

would not have thought it easy to change—of the Prince who turned a dwarf into a warrior!"

"What is this?"

He told her the story of Hans. She listened and turned to me.

"There, Luke! If you can break one custom you can break another."

"It is not the same thing."

"In what way is it different?"

I tried to explain, but stumbled over my words. One was a question of making good a pledge, of honor. No question of honor was involved in the other. Custom must hold except under a stronger compulsion.

They contested me eagerly, stumbling not over their own words but each other's in their anxiety to prove me wrong. They were both much readier tongued than I was, and their combined attack, with Edmund reinforcing Blodwen and Blodwen putting Edmund's argument again but more sharply, overwhelmed me. I did my best, doggedly, to maintain my stand.

Edmund said, laughing: "The one thing he really believes in is the Prince's will. This Prince's will, anyway! He will break the customs he wants to break, and nobly uphold the rest."

"The Prince's will, indeed!" Blodwen said. "And what of the Princess's? Does my will count for nothing?"

"Not against this tyrant," Edmund said. "But if you beg it of him prettily, he may grant it you as a favor. It is worth trying."

They were both laughing. In mock humility Blodwen dropped to her knees and bowed her head.

"My Lord," she said, the tone piteous, "will you grant your handmaiden, out of your greatness and nobility, this humble plea?"

I lifted her to her feet, laughing myself. "You will soil your gown."

"Not in Winchester," she said. "Your floors may be of plain wood but I notice they are well scrubbed. Well, Luke?"

"You can have your way," I said, "though Strohan, my butler, will very likely die of shock when he hears. The ladies will be at the banquet."

"Good!" she said. "I look forward to seeing them. I think a man may be well judged by his lady. I am anxious to see Edmund's."

"I have none," he said.

Her eyes widened. "Not even one in prospect?"

"I have been kept too busy by Luke, what with expeditions into the barbarous north and battles against the city's enemies."

"But you must bring someone, now that the great Prince has given way to us!"

"I can bring my sister, I suppose."

"Then do so! A sister may tell one something about a man as well. Perhaps more than his lady could."

I watched them and was happy. I did not mind being bested in such a thing as this and by such a pair: my betrothed bride and my best friend.

She could charm anyone when she set out to. I need not have worried about Strohan; he was already her besotted slave. The banquet was a great success and so were all the other receptions, whether at the palace or in visiting the city's nobles. People opened to her, like flowers to the visiting sun.

And since she was not one of those who put on a show, of ceremony or graciousness, she was as winning in small intimate gatherings as in more formal ones. She was interested in the diversity of mankind, and loved to hear men talk of their ideas and beliefs. With Blodwen to draw them out, they talked readily enough.

She said one day something about asking someone to join us for supper in her apartments and I nodded absently. My mind at that time was preoccupied with a captaincy that had fallen vacant and the various claims of those who should be considered for the place. She said:

"I must make inquiries in case there are things he cannot eat. In my country the Christians do not eat meat on one day in the week. They may have some such rule here also."

"Not eat meat? But if they are Christians I suppose it does not matter: they do not have to swing a sword." I realized, belatedly, what she had said. "But you are not asking Christians to dine here?"

She said, scolding: "You have not been listening to what I said. Not just Christians. Their Bishop."

"But you cannot do so, Blodwen," I said. " I know little of the Christians in your country, but here they are despised and rightly. They are a crazed lot, always talking about this dead god of theirs. They were useful to the city once, when Peter led the army through their secret tunnel, but that has been well paid for. Not only in gold, and now in land, but also in boredom during the time my brother was Prince and they had access to the palace."

"He is not being asked to the palace," she said, "but to my apartment as my guest." I shrugged in resignation, realizing that her mind was made up, and she smiled at me. "You will come, won't you, Luke? I have asked your friend Martin as well, so you can talk to him if the boredom proves too great."

"Martin! But he is an Acolyte. You cannot ask him to meet a Christian."

She smiled again, very sweetly. "I have already done so. And he has said yes."

I had seen the Bishop once or twice in the city. Even apart from the black gown he wore and the wooden cross he hung around his neck, he was distinctive in appearance. The priest who counseled Ann and consoled Peter after her death had been a small, weak-looking creature with a stoop. The Bishop was big and broad, with powerful arms and hands and a strong wide face. Like the priest his head was shaved except for a thin circle of hair above the ears, but his huge skull had such a polish on it that I doubted if any hair grew there in the first place.

His voice matched his frame, being deep and booming. He spoke as someone sure of himself, and laughed readily. And however he may have behaved among his lunatic followers, with us he talked in a rational fashion. He spoke of the city, which he said he had long wished to see, and told us things concerning its past, before the Disaster, which were new to me. I had learned from the Seers that there had once been kings and queens in the great city called London, who had ruled all England and territories beyond the oceans as well. The Bishop told us that in still earlier days English kings had ruled not from London but from this city of Winchester. It may have been no more than a fanciful tale, but he told it convincingly.

He did not say anything about his Christian god until Blodwen put questions to him, but then he told that tale well also. It was the wildest fantasy, this story of the maker of the whole universe being born in a stable, living as a man and dying a painful and degrading death, but he described it so well that for the moment one could almost believe it.

But Martin said: "You have not told all, Bishop." There was anger in his voice. "You have not spoken of his mother being a virgin, or a star moving through the sky to lead kings to worship him."

The Bishop said: "These things are less important."

"Are they? Your Christians do not think so. Nor do I. Truth does not surround itself with lies."

"You speak warmly, Acolyte," the Bishop said. "You are a devotee of truth?"

"I know of no better thing to seek."

"And do you find it in the darkness of your Seance Hall, when the Spirits speak with the tongues of men?" His voice was amused, and I saw Martin's face flush. "But let us keep to abstract matters. There was a poet in ancient days who wrote about truth. He said:

> "'Beauty is truth, truth beauty. That is all
> Ye know on earth, and all ye need to know.'"

Martin stared at him. "It is well said."

"Well said, but he gives himself the lie. His words are beautiful but they are not true. Truth can be ugly."

"I deny that!"

"Do you? Listen. A good woman lies dying. She asks after her son. The truth is that he is a convicted felon and will be hanged in the morning. Will you tell her so? Truth which lacks pity is a cruel thing, and where there is cruelty there can be no beauty."

Martin said: "The poet spoke of the nature of things, not of men's speech."

"Is not men's speech part of the nature of things? What men do matters more than what they know. Our ancestors had wonderful machines." I started at that word; even to use it was improper. "Men turned against them because it was machines, through the agency of evil spirits, that caused the Disaster."

The Bishop smiled. "At any rate, that is what the Seers tell us. I am glad myself that the machines are gone but for a different reason. Machines put a distance between men. A man could give an order on one side of the world and command obedience on the other. Our Prince here must earn obedience, from men he sees and who see him. In those days a man could press a button and kill a thousand men a thousand miles away. We Christians, as you know, do not accept any kind of killing, but if killing there must be I would rather it were done by a warrior who kills with his own hand, and knows what bloody corpse he leaves behind."

I did not like this talk of forbidden things. I would have ordered him to be silent, even though he was a guest of Blodwen's, but she herself spoke first. She said:

"The old days are dead and gone and it does no good to talk of them. And of course you are right, Bishop, to say that one does not tell harsh truths to someone not strong enough to bear them. But it is a better case when people have that strength."

"It may be better," the Bishop said, "but it is not a common thing."

"Not among your Christians, maybe," I said.

He shook his head. "Not even among warriors."

They were good days, passing lightly, and quickly. I forgot the doubts which Blodwen's words had put into my mind on that first evening in the palace. And she did not speak in such a way again. If she had seemed unhappy I might have been troubled. But she was content, and that contented me.

I remember a day in high summer when we went

in boats on the river. There were no more than a dozen of us in the party, all young. We went down river, scarcely needing to row because the current took us. It was a fine morning, the sky blue and white, the sun hot when it pierced the clouds. We went a long way, past Twyford, and on to the place where the river meanders through a broad valley of water meadows.

We picnicked there and then lay idly on the grass of the river bank, the boats moored and bobbing beside us, and talked and laughed and were pleasantly idle. We were on our own, with no servants even, and I could lay aside the cares and countenance of a Prince. Apart from Blodwen there were three other girls, one of them Jenny. They were pretty enough in their summer dresses. But compared with Blodwen they were daisies to a rose.

Her dress was green, with long full sleeves. It was a Wilsh cloth, more brightly hued than any we had in the south. Its brightness made the grass look dull, as her beauty made the other girls seem plain.

We had no minstrels either, but Edmund and Matthew Grant had brought their lutes. They played them for our amusement, and Edmund sang. He had a good voice, high but sweet and true. One of his songs was "The Miller of Dee," and Blodwen, applauding it, said:

"We have that same song in my country! In fact it is said that he lived beside the river higher up the valley in which Klan Gothlen lies. It is called the Dee."

Edmund laughed. "And do you have this song also?"

His fingers plucked the strings in a slow haunting tune. He sang:

"Oh Greensleeves was all my joy,
Greensleeves was my delight,
Greensleeves was my heart of gold,
And who but Lady Greensleeves?"

She clapped her hands and said: "I have heard it, but never so well sung, I think. You should be a minstrel, Edmund."

I laughed. "I cannot spare him, though! I have more need of him as a warrior."

It was not long after that the cares of state caught up with me again. Horsemen came riding toward us

along the river bank. It was Greene with a small troop.
The pigeons had brought word from Romsey: there
was trouble there. It had been put down and the garrison was in no danger, but Greene had thought it
best to tell me.

He had had the sense also to bring a spare mount.
We were almost as near Romsey as Winchester. I
said:

"We had better ride over and make sure."

Blodwen protested: "Do not spoil such a day as
this, Luke! He has told you there is no danger."

I hesitated, but said: "No, I must go, my love.
There will be other days to enjoy. Edmund will row
you back for me. Will you not, Edmund?"

"As my Prince commands," he said, "though I
would point out that it will be against the stream. I
shall expect a good wage for such heavy work."

We laughed, and I said to Blodwen: "Give him
his supper, and a pot of ale to cool him."

"You will not be back this night?"

I shook my head. "I think not. But tomorrow,
certain."

I looked back as we rode away. Blodwen sat with
her knees drawn up and her small hands clasped over

them. Edmund stood by her, playing the lute and singing. It was a fine scene and I was reluctant to leave it. But as I had said, there would be other days.

Martin came to see me in the palace one night a few weeks after this. He wasted no time, but said:

"I have come to say good-by."

"Good-by!" I was astonished. "You are not leaving us?"

He nodded. I thought how absurd he looked with his tonsured head and spectacles above the Acolyte's black cloak. It was hard to believe that he had once fought at my side in the Contest. But despite the absurdity, perhaps because of it, I felt an uprush of affection for him.

I said: "To go where?"

"To Sanctuary."

"But for how long?"

"I don't know. Perhaps for good."

"You cannot do that, Martin," I said. "Visit your High Seers, if you must, and see their wonders. But then come back to me. They can offer nothing to make up for having to live underground like a mole, with neither sunlight nor fresh air." I spoke with more confidence, remembering my own time in Sanctuary and how I had chafed against its confinement and restrictions. "You could not do it. It is different for the High Seers. They are old men but you are young."

"I cannot stay here. I cannot go on with the trickery and deception and lies in the Seance Hall. The end may be good but I cannot tolerate these means. That Christian Bishop mocked me for it and I had no answer."

I said: "He will bear watching, that one. He knows too much and speaks too freely. I have warned Grimm of it. But if this is all your problem, it is easily solved. I told you once before I could rid you of that black dress if you wished. It is still more true now. I have only to say a word to Grimm and you are dispensed from the vows you took."

He smiled, but with no joy. "And what shall I do then? I am no warrior and would prove a poor courtier."

"You can be my friend and counselor, as you were when we were boys together. If you desire an office I can call you Chancellor, as Cymru calls Snake, the polymuf who advises him."

"And if I advised you to give Petersfield and Romsey back to their citizens? You need no counselor, Luke."

"I need friends."

"It is no good. Not much more than a year ago I hung in chains, with faggots round my feet, and men with torches ready to light them. You saved me, but it marks one to watch a hard and ugly death draw close. I must do something with the life you gave back to me, and it is not enough to sit at court and be your friend."

I could not follow his thoughts. A man faced death, but when death drew back forgot it until the next time. But there was a desperation in his face. I felt suddenly cold. I had friends already, and Blodwen, but I did not want to lose him. Yet I would make no plea. I said:

"So be it. The Spirits go with you."

FOUR

THE PLAYER KING

A T THE TIME OF THE AUTUMN FAIR, WITH the campaigns over and the fields harvested, we held a great ball in Blodwen's honor. I sent the pigeons far and wide and got fair answer. The Princes of Guildford and Basingstroke, Alton and Andover and Salisbury came to us as guests. Strohan was in desperation, finding room for them all in the palace. And the Prince of Oxford sent his son.

Oxford was a city of great power and influence, ruling much territory. Towns as remote as Marlborough, more than thirty miles away across hilly country, stood under its sovereignty. The Seers must have thought of this city before they chose Winchester as the pivot of their plan. I guessed that their reason for rejecting it was because it lay remote, on the edge of the civilized lands, while we lay at the heart. Their northern border was the Burning Lands. Under that smoking sky, livid with flame by night, they were remote in a different sense: they were a sullen people, content to keep to themselves. Probably that was another reason why the Seers had looked elsewhere.

Our armies had never met theirs in the field, and there had never before been a royal visit. I knew why this invitation had been accepted. I ruled three cities now from Winchester. Even in the remoteness of Oxford that was something to cause sober thought. The Prince had sent his son to take a close look at me and my city.

I was prepared to be treated warily, and to treat him warily in return. He was a few years older than I, and had been heir to his father's throne all his life. I expected an aloof unfriendly man, mindful of the power I had won but at the same time despising me as an upstart. When the Seer of Oxford named him

Prince in Waiting, my father had been a common Sergeant, not yet ennobled.

But my anticipation went much amiss. His name was Eric and in character he gave the lie to his townsmen's reputation. He was olive-skinned, handsome apart from a broken nose and the scar of a sword slash on the side of his neck, and he smiled easily. He talked easily too, in the drawling accent of his city.

I could see that he was setting himself out to please me, and at first my wariness was reinforced by this. But I found there was more to him than charm: much more. When we sat alone together in my parlor, he talked good sense and with frankness.

He said: "You will know why I have come, Luke. Your reputation has traveled far, and grown as it traveled. Old stories are recalled. Of a Seance, for instance, where you were named as one who would be Prince of Princes. Men fear you for what you have achieved, and might yet achieve."

I watched him, making no comment on this. He said:

"I came expecting to find someone crazed with power and vainglory, to hunt out his weaknesses against a future conflict. I find you a reasonable man. I think our minds may not lie far apart. We are both young. We both look for change from old and stupid ways."

He smiled. "It is far worse, I think, in Oxford than in Winchester. Nothing can be done there that was not done last year. My father is not a bad man, but stern and inflexible. As a child I earned a few thrashings for not obeying the rules. After that I learned to give them lip service, and keep my own counsel.

"But it is time there was change. As I say, the stories of Luke of Winchester run fast, in and out of many cities, and reach us, too. Stories of your journey to the north, where you killed the Bayemot, and stories of your conquests. But there is one I have only heard since I came here: of how you decreed a dwarf should be a warrior. I like that one. It gives a different ring to all the others."

I did not disappoint him by telling him I had done it to keep a pledge rather than to bring about change for its own sake. And though I believed him honest I could not tell him the secrets of the Seers. But here was someone who might be a strong ally when the time was ripe. He himself put it into words:

"I have fought with our army and will again if there is need. But these battles achieve nothing, serve no useful purpose. The time for petty rulers is over. We need a single government to give laws throughout the land. I think I have fathomed your aim, and if I have I agree with it. I can do nothing while my father lives, but he is an old man and sick. When I can help, I will."

I said: "I believe you, Eric. And this is good to hear."

"One other thing. You will not find me jealous of your glory. I seek only to be your lieutenant. When the time comes I will gladly bend a knee to the Prince of Princes."

It was not in my nature to trust any but a well-tried friend, and I had learned enough of the princely craft, and of the lies and intrigues that surround it, not to be deceived by fair words and smiles. I would not relax my guard with Eric of Oxford, as my father so fatally had done with Fat Jeremy. But though I would keep my precautions I did believe him honest. And liked him also.

It would serve all my ends to bind him closer to

us. As it happened, there was something which could help bring that about. He met my Captains and their Ladies, among them Edmund's sister, Jenny. And it was plain that he was taken with her.

Thereafter I took care that they were thrown together. He was, I knew, unmarried and unbetrothed, as she was. He was happy to be in Winchester, free of the gloom and protocol of Oxford. In this mood he might be glad to take a girl of this city back with him as a bride. And it would suit me very well to have him do so.

Nor was Jenny a person to whom even the Prince of Oxford could object as a future lady for his son. She came of a family that had been noble for generations—since the Disaster—and her father had been Prince of Winchester. It would be a good match.

I told only Blodwen of my hopes. She did not dispute the advantages, but said:

"I think you will find him eager enough. I am not so sure of her."

"But she likes him. Anyone can see she does. Did you not see them laughing together only this morning?"

Blodwen smiled. "Liking is not loving."

"His looks are good enough. He is a tried warrior. He is cheerful and has a nimble wit. And he is a Prince's son, Prince in Waiting to a great city. What more could she want?"

"Poor Luke! You know how to wage war or make a treaty, but in the trivial small maze of a woman's mind you are lost utterly. Jenny does not need telling any of that; she sees it before you do. But if she does not have a heart to give, it is no help."

"But she is not betrothed!"

"No," Blodwen said, "she is not betrothed." She sighed. "I will not argue with you. Perhaps it will fall out as you hope. Luke, I must go. There is a last fitting for my gown for tonight. I do not want to disgrace you at the ball."

I was with Jenny when Blodwen came into the Hall of Mirrors. There was a sudden hush in the talk. I recalled a similar silence falling on the Wilsh court in Cymru's throne room, the night I saw her first, and turned to look.

She had brought her other dresses with her, but this one had been made by our Winchester tailors.

The cloth was silk, less fine and less brightly dyed than that of the Wilsh: a dull crimson. But to make up for it they had put heavy gold braid at the neck and hem and on the deep cuffs. And they had cut it cunningly so that it clung close to her, and yet swirled from her as she walked.

I said, involuntarily: "By the Great, have you ever seen anything so lovely?"

"No," Jenny said. Her voice was small. "Nothing."

"I must go to her," I said. "And I think Eric is looking for you, Jenny."

"Then I suppose I must wait here until he finds me."

She turned away, and I went to Blodwen. I was almost afraid to touch her when we stood up together for the first dance, but she took my hand firmly with her small warm one, and tugged me sharply into line when I made a false step. I had never had much skill in these enterprises.

Apart from that, things went well. I saw Eric dancing with Jenny, and that pleased me. Later I saw him go out with her through the open doors into the garden, which pleased me still more. Then, just before supper, I saw Eric on his own.

I said: "Are you looking for Jenny? I think I saw her . . ."

He cut across my words, an unusual impoliteness.

"No." He looked unhappy. "I'm sorry, Luke." He put on a smile but it was more rueful than cheerful. "I have suffered a reverse."

"A reverse? How?"

He told me. He had proposed marriage to her and been refused. And it was clear, though he did not charge her with it, that the refusal had been brusque rather than gentle.

My anger rose. I knew that hardness of Jenny's. In the past I had suffered from it. She had the right to take her own decisions, but no right to be rude to a friend of mine, a Prince I looked to as an ally.

I made excuses and left him. I looked for Jenny and soon found her. I said:

"A private word with you."

She smiled but her lips were tight. "As you wish, sire."

The garden was the nearest place. There was an arbor beyond the sundial and we had it to ourselves. We could hear the minstrels' music and see figures moving in the Hall of Mirrors, but at this spot it was quiet and private.

Jenny said: "This is the second time I have been brought here tonight."

Her voice was provocative and defiant. My anger increased. I told her what I thought of her conduct. Eric was a good man. He did not deserve to be treated with contempt.

"And did he say I did so treat him?"

"No. But he was hurt. If a woman must refuse a man she can do it decently, without wounding him."

She was silent; then said: "I did not mean to hurt him. I agree, he is a good man. But he took me by surprise, and I am not . . . accustomed to such things." I saw her look at me in the dark. "If you think it right, Luke, I will tell him I am sorry."

She had accepted the rebuke and was trying to make amends. In a calmer mood I would have realized this, and let it go. But my anger was not only on Eric's behalf. It stemmed also from the frustration of my plans. I said savagely:

"You are a fool, as well. You will get no better offer than this, nor one a tenth as good."

She stared at me. Fire came back into her voice too. She said:

"A Prince may command his people. But by what right does he tell them how to live their lives?"

"For your own good! Because you are blind, girl, to your own interest."

"Blind?" She laughed. "As blind as the Prince of Winchester?"

We faced each other in bitterness and rage. I saw the rapid rise and fall of her breast and my own pulse was racing. In the distance there was the soft murmur of voices, above the music of a minuet. I said:

"I have eyes that can tell a fool, and a friend."

"Have you? And a betrothed bride who dallies with a friend? Can they tell that?"

I laughed now. "You are not just a fool, but mad."

Her voice dropped but was burning still. "Yours are the only eyes that do not see it."

I took her arm roughly, my fingers bruising the flesh. She winced and I said:

"You tell this lie of Blodwen. I could have you whipped for that and may do yet, noble though you are. But what man do you traduce? What friend do you call false?"

"You know it. You do not need telling."

It was true. In such a catalogue of lies there could only be one name. I said:

"Edmund?"

She stared in silence and the silence gave assent. I let go her arm.

"So you charge your own brother with this. You disgust me. Without a single jot of evidence."

My contempt provoked her again.

"Listen," she said, "listen, blind Luke. Do you remember a day when we picnicked in the water meadows, and you were called away to Romsey? Edmund took her back in your place. Not to the city only but to her apartments. And stayed there after."

"At my bidding. I told Blodwen to give him his supper, in return for the rowing."

Jenny said: "They dined late that night. I went to his room after eleven, and he was not there."

"You speak out of narrowness and ignorance. The Wilsh love talking late into the night. In Klan Gothlen Edmund and I have sat with Cymru till two of the morning. Eleven is late by our standards but not by theirs."

She said nothing. In the distance the music stopped

and the chatter of voices swelled up. I said:

"Exile would be better than whipping. I would rather not see your face again. But to take any action would injure Edmund. So go your way, Jenny, and keep out of mine."

She went without speaking by the path that would take her from the palace. I walked, willing myself to calmness, back to the Hall of Mirrors. Another dance had struck up as I got there. Edmund stood opposite Blodwen. They saw me look at them, and smiled.

A troop of players came to us that winter. They were not the ordinary strolling players, who acted their parts in any room large enough, or in the open air, and sent one of their numbers round with a greasy cap to collect money off their audience. These were more ambitious. In Salisbury they had had what they called a theater, and they took a disused malt-house to make a similar place in our city. It was in the River Road, not far from my Aunt Mary's house.

This was one more sign of how Winchester's importance was growing in men's eyes. Players, like thieves and tricksters, will always flock where there are full pockets to be emptied, and they had heard talk of our wealth and prosperity. But it was not just a question of money. Their chief player and manager, a lean arrogant man in his thirties with a black pointed beard and showy dress, let it be known that they had come because it was fitting that the greatest city should have the greatest company of players.

This swaggering was typical of him. When he paid his respects to me and to my Captains, he brought his hat down in a bow that caused the feather on top of it to sweep the floor, but the gesture was empty. He made it plain that in truth he thought little of warriors or nobles, or anyone who did not belong to his own seedy profession. And that in that profession he believed that no other could come near him. I had never met even a Prince with such overweening pride.

Of my own inclination I would have sent him packing back to Salisbury. But his reputation had traveled ahead of him. The people were anxious to see these players, and it was true that if they were any good they would help relieve the winter's tedium. Blodwen spoke for them also. She had been used to plays and theaters in her own city, and missed these diversions.

So they set to work to turn the malt-house to their ends, and dwarfs worked busily under the direction of this man who called himself, in further illustration of his modesty, the Player King. At last it was finished, and news of the first play cried in the streets. His messenger came to the palace, humbly inviting me and my court to be present at the opening.

We arrived as a gray evening was turning into a hard black night. Snow which had threatened all day had not yet come, but the frost was sharp. A knifing wind blew from the east.

Inside braziers had been set up and it was less cold, but we still had need of our cloaks. The dwarfs had done their work well, and I acknowledged that the direction had been good. The walls had been brightly painted, and the ceiling also. And the floor had been constructed to be on three levels. The highest part was at the back where there were benches; for the common people, but empty now. Then came the section where chairs were set out for us. Below that again was the part they called the stage. A heavy curtain, draped from ceiling to floor, covered the front of it.

When we were seated the Player King came. He said to me:

"Are you comfortable, sire?"

There was that in his voice which suggested that our discomfort would insult him. I said:

"Well enough. And it is a fine theater. Though some might think it strange that you set the commons above their betters."

He smiled. "Would you rather they came between you and the stage? As it is, if they were not raised up they would see little of the play. And you must remember, sire, that in the realm of dream and imagination all men are equal." He bowed. "It is our privilege to offer a place in which even a Prince can put aside both cares and crown for an hour in exchange for the airy stuff of fantasy."

He said it glibly. What was not said because no saying was needed was that not all in fact were equal here: others must yield to the authority of the Player King. I said shortly:

"What play will you give us?"

"It is called 'Tristram and Iseult,'" he said. "I have written it myself, though the story is ancient." He bowed again. "And if you are ready, sire, we will waste no further time."

He pulled his cloak about him and went through

the curtains onto the stage. Soon after that the curtains drew away to either side. Some of the ladies exclaimed with pleasure. In front of us was the representation of a throne room. There were two thrones, painted to look like gold, and other gaudy trappings. Although the space was small, the eye was deceived into seeing grandeur there. Side walls had pillars cunningly painted on them, and at the back a painted window looked out and down to crags in a bright blue sea. It was the palace of a great king, set high on a seagirt cliff. And into the throne room from a door at one side, his cloak thrown off to show a dress of garish magnificence and a golden crown on his head, strode the Player King.

He played the part of Mark, king of this imaginary country. The story told how Mark had a lieutenant and friend called Tristram, whom he sent on his behalf to request the hand of the daughter of the king in a land called Ire. The contract was made and Tristram brought Iseult, the daughter, back with him to Mark's court.

Iseult's mother, seeking to ensure her daughter's happiness, gave a love potion to the serving maid who was to go with her. This was to be given to

Mark before the wedding, and would ensure that he loved her all his days. But Tristram and Iseult, not knowing what it was, found the flask with the potion and drank it together. So they must love each other, as long as they should live.

A strange uneasiness grew in me as this tale unfolded. I had expected to be bored, never having had much taste for minstrels or mummers, but this was not boredom. I felt a sickness in my stomach, a tightness in my chest as though a giant's hand gripped my heart.

A scene came in which, with long poetic speeches, Tristram and Iseult declared their love but swore to fight against it. Tristram was Mark's friend, Iseult his affianced bride. They knew they loved each other but they would not betray him. And as they talked on the stage they drew closer together and then, still swearing they would never yield to love, embraced and kissed.

It was a moment of high drama. All eyes, it seemed, were fixed upon the players. But my eyes went to Blodwen. I saw her look not at the stage but at Edmund; and as though word had gone silently from heart to heart his eyes met hers. For a long moment they locked, then turned away.

The sickness and tightness grew worse, and coldness was added to them. My legs shivered. I had to clamp my jaw tight to keep my teeth from chattering.

I had tried to put aside all thought of what Jenny had said in the garden. If by chance the memory came to me I dismissed it. Now all flooded back. I heard the soft music again in the distance and heard her voice, hard with contempt: "Listen . . . Listen, blind Luke . . ."

The play ran its course. I saw nothing in it but resemblances. Tristram was a skilled player of the harp and sang a love song to Iseult. I thought of Edmund playing his lute in the water meadows and singing: "Greensleeves was all my joy, Greensleeves was my delight . . ." The Player King made Mark a man stupidly blind to what was happening, concerned only with the affairs of state, a dull and heavy creature. I saw myself riding away to Romsey, leaving the pleasant scene behind.

And there rage supplanted sickness. Jenny had said: "Yours are the only eyes that do not see it." Could that be true? Could the fact of my betrayal be as clear as Mark's was? Was it the talk of Winchester?

The Player King had said he had written the play himself. Were these things jibes at me?

I had an urge to leap down onto the stage, to knock aside the wooden sword the Player King wore with my steel one, and spit him with it. But as always my mind worked coldly behind my rage. There might be killing needed yet, but this was not the time.

The play ended somehow. Mark killed Tristram, I think, and Iseult stabbed herself. I was only concerned that it should be over. The players paraded for our applause and then the Player King came to me again, and asked if their poor efforts had met with my approval.

"It was entertaining," I said, "as these things go."

He bowed stiffly, disconcerted. Blodwen said:

"Oh, it was good! We have no better players in Klan Gothlen. And the play was finely written. Luke, you must reward him well."

I saw her face, candid and eager, and could not believe her false. Behind her Edmund smiled at me, as he had done many times, over her enthusiasm. If they were not honest the whole world was a stinking ruin, broken and slimed like the village which the

Bayemot overran. And I had killed the Bayemot. I said to the Player King:

"You played well. Gold will be sent you in the morning."

But in the night I woke, and having wakened did not sleep again. Scenes from the play came back to me; the words of the two lovers rang in my ears with Jenny's mocking voice behind them. "Listen . . . Listen, blind Luke . . ." I tossed and turned and, rising early, took a horse and rode out of the North Gate, past the astonished watch.

I rode hard and far, like a coward fleeing from a battlefield. But there was no escaping this battle; its blind and hateful warriors harried me without mercy, and a hundred swords pierced me. And I knew there was no medicine to heal these wounds.

So I came back, tired and sick at heart, to the city which I ruled. I had become a slave to my own eyes and ears. I must watch them both, listen to every word that passed between them, interpret every gesture. While I did so, I must hide my misery.

And in my slavery I was tossed to and fro. I would see her look at him and fill with anger. Then she would look at me, wide-eyed and smiling, and the anger would turn to love, and self-disgust. I had no interest in anything else. My Captains came to me, with news or questions, and I listened and spoke and a moment later did not know what they had said or I had replied.

Days passed. I had no appetite but forced myself to eat, dully chewing and swallowing the food which like everything else but one thing had become meaningless. My life was consumed with watching, guessing. Then one night, when we had both been guests in his mother's house, he handed her her cloak on parting and I saw his hand rest, for another long moment, on her shoulder.

We walked through the streets toward the palace; for so short a distance we had not brought horses. They were less dark than they had been: last winter I had had oil lamps put up such as they had in Salisbury. Blodwen hummed a tune. I said:

"Are you happy?"

"Yes!"

"Are you thinking yet of returning to Klan Gothlen?"

She glanced at me in surprise. "Why, no."

"You have been a long time here."

She laughed. "Have I outstayed my welcome, then?"

"If you do not go soon, you will be caught by the winter."

"Would that be so terrible a thing?"

I said slowly: "I was wondering . . . what it is that keeps you."

"I have told you. I love your city. More than my own, I think."

I said: "What person?"

"What person? Who else but Luke, Prince of Three Cities?"

She said the words lightly, jesting, but there was a falseness. I asked:

"What of Edmund?"

"I am fond of Edmund, and all your friends."

"Only fond?"

She stopped. We stood under an oil lamp. Some distance away a polymuf scuttled into an alley, made still more crooked in shape by the shadows which surrounded him. We were alone. Blodwen said:

"Speak openly, Luke, and honestly."

My throat swelled and I had to force words from it.

"This," I said. "Have you betrayed me with Edmund?"

Her eyes looked into mine unflinchingly. "I have not betrayed you with Edmund, or anyone."

My misery lifted. I could live again as a free man, not a fugitive from nightmares. I said:

"You swear this?"

"If swearing is needed, I swear it."

I wanted only one thing more. I took her hands.

"And you do not love him? You will swear that, too?"

She smiled, and for the instant all was well. Then she shook her head.

"No," she said softly. "That I will not swear."

FIVE

THE COUNCIL OF CAPTAINS

I SENT WORD VERY EARLY TO EDMUND THAT I wished him to ride with me. It was still dark when we clattered down the High Street, drawing curses from an upper room where the noise of our passing roused some good citizen from sleep, across the river and along the road to East Gate.

He asked me when we met what reason there was for our journey, at such an hour. I told him he would know in good time. It had crossed my mind that Blodwen might have sent word to him herself, telling him of what had passed between us, and I searched his face for sign of this. But the bewilderment there was real; he truly did not know why I had come for him. He shrugged his shoulders and, accepting his Prince's command as a Captain must, mounted and rode with me.

The guard saluted us as we left the city. I set no frenzied pace as I had done on that recent solitary ride. Then my adversaries had been phantasms of the mind. Now there was only one, who had a face and rode at my side. The sky ahead was paling with the dawn. I looked behind me at the gate and remembered my father's head, stuck on a spear above it. I had thought life could bring no greater anguish than that. It seemed a small thing now.

We traveled in silence. Edmund was not unused to this. I had had my times of silence before, when my mind was busy with some project and I saw no need of speech, and he had accustomed himself to them. The city slept behind us. There was only the sound of hoofs and harness and our horses' breaths snorting in the chilly air.

We reached the Elder Pond, black and rimmed with ice, and I took the fork that led to the Contest Field. I reined my horse in when we reached it. It lay bare and empty, with the dark mass of Catherine's Hill behind it. On the hill's top its grove of trees stood like mourners against the ashen sky. I thought of this place as I had seen it once, with the sun shining after rain on a spring day, and the whole city, it seemed, cheering the Young Captains as they led their teams in for the Contest.

There had been something to win then, too, and against great odds. I remembered my young self. Had I fought so hard for no more than a jeweled sword?

Edmund kept the silence. I said at last:

"Do you recall the time we fought here?"

"Of course."

"And how I beat you."

He smiled. "That, too."

"You said once, when we watched another Contest together, that on a second chance you would have won."

"Did I, Luke?" He shook his head. "I do not remember that."

"Do you still think so?"

"That I would have beaten you? No. I knew that after you had killed the Bayemot. I have some courage but when the odds are hopeless I draw back. You would always beat me; not so much because you are a better fighter as because you will not accept defeat."

I paused before I said: "At least some good came of it."

"Yes. You rule three cities, and will rule more."

I said: "Our friendship."

"Yes. A better thing still."

"It has meant much to me. I have Captains who serve me well, a dwarf warrior who would die for me, but those things are not friendship. There were three of us: you, Martin and I. Martin turned Acolyte and now has left us altogether, to go to Sanctuary. Only you and I remain."

There was a faraway honking and high up small dots trailed across the gray. Wild geese, on their journey to lands we would never know. I said:

"Let us talk of Blodwen, Edmund."

Our eyes met. He said slowly: "What of her?"

"I think you know."

He did not deny that, but said: "There has been nothing between us."

"Nothing?" I spoke bitterly. "No looks, no touches of hands?"

"No more than that."

"Listen," I said, "she is mine. Cymru gave her to me at the banquet at which we both sat, after the killing of the Bayemot. Is this not true?"

"Yes," Edmund said. "But she is a girl, not something to be given."

In the mind's eye I saw Blodwen again, as she stood with me on the staircase above her father's throne room, and heard her voice: "I am not an honor—I am Blodwen! I will be my own woman. Remember that, Luke of Winchester." I said:

"Is it the office of a friend to come between a man and his betrothed bride, even with a single look?"

Then he looked ashamed. He said in a low voice:

"It was not meant. I promise you."

"You could not help it?"

"No."

"Perhaps you could not. I do not think I blame you. But you are a free man. You can make an end of it now."

He did not speak. I said:

"I claim this for our friendship's sake."

The wind blew cold down Catherine's Hill and

our horses stamped their feet. Edmund spoke at last.

"I will end it."

I reached across and clasped his arm. "I will not forget this! And now, I have a mission for you."

He looked startled. "A mission?"

"To Oxford. To talk in public with its Prince; in private with its Prince in Waiting. I look for two alliances, one open, the other secret."

Edmund said: "How long will the mission last?"

"I will expect you back in the spring. We will watch the Contest of the Young Captains together."

"And when would you have me go?"

"Today."

"Be open with me," he said. "It is because of Blodwen that I am to be sent away? Such a mission would be best in older hands than mine."

"You have been too free with her. This you admit. You said you could not help it and I believe you. All things wither without nourishment. It is better that you do not see her for a time."

I twitched my horse's rein, turning her head back toward the city. Edmund said: "Hold, Luke."

"Well?"

"Have you spoken to Blodwen of this?"

It might have been better to lie, but I could not. "Yes."

"What did you say to her?"

"I asked her if she had betrayed me with you. She swore she had not. I knew she spoke truth."

"And what else?"

I echoed him: "What else?"

His voice had changed. There was boldness in it.

"You put a question to her and got your answer. But still you need to send me away to Oxford. Is it only my weakness you fear? What reassurance did you seek from Blodwen, and not find?"

I said: "What passes between Blodwen and me is our concern, not yours."

"You are wrong, Luke! I will not go on your mission until I have put a question to her. And if her answer is what I think it may be, then you must find another man for Oxford."

I felt cold again: a cold sharper and more inward than that which the wind scoured from the ugly sky.

"You will not try to take her from me."

"Not unless she puts out a hand to me. But if she does, nothing will stop me taking it."

"Not friendship?"

"Not anything!"

He spoke exultantly. I said:

"And if I beg you?"

All my body trembled. I felt tears start in my eyes, and blinked them back.

He said: "Do not beg for something which I cannot give."

"Cannot, or will not?"

"What difference is there? There are strengths beyond our own."

I said, wonderingly, to myself almost: "I never doubted your loyalty. I would have doubted my own sooner. I know my weaknesses and I gave you best in friendship. But I could not do such injury to a friend. I would die first."

The day was lighter, and I saw him flush. He said:

"You are my friend, but Blodwen I love. There is a difference in our natures. I do not think you have ever truly loved. Or ever could."

"I loved you," I said, "who were my friend."

He shook his head. "Talking does no good."

"Listen," I said. "Forget friendship, if it means so little to you. Have you thought of the harm that can come from this? Not just to us, but to the city."

"You have got your city," he said. "Keep it. We do not want it."

He linked her desires with his, as though of right. Pain raked its claws through me. I said:

"Even if I would, I could not let you have her. I am Prince of the city and she, daughter of the King of the Wilsh, is to be my bride. If it is not held to I am no Prince, and chaos follows."

"Then let it follow. You cannot stop us, Luke."

"I am Prince," I said. "I have some powers."

We rode together back to the city and in silence. The guard saluted us again at the East Gate, and I bade him bring the Sergeant. He was out of the guardhouse on the instant. His name was Tunney, one of Harding's men, old for a warrior but still powerful. I pointed to Edmund.

"Arrest him."

Blodwen said: "Luke, what have you done?"

Her face was white and she showed signs of haste. She had come unannounced to where I sat in my parlor. It was early still. Outside the window a few small flakes of snow drifted slowly down.

I said: "In what way, lady?"

"They say that Edmund is under guard. Because of what I said last night? I promise you . . ."

I thought she might lie, to save him, and did not want to hear it. I cut across her words.

"I gave an order to a Captain and he refused to obey it. That is all and that is enough."

"What order?"

I told her of the mission to Oxford. Her eyes were on my face as I spoke, and I watched her watching me. At the end she said only:

"What will you do to him?"

"A Prince must have obedience from his Captains, in peace as much as in war. You know this. Disobedience imperils the city and merits death. But I will do him no harm. I will only banish him."

"You cannot do it, Luke."

"I must," I said, "or see a man walking the streets of Winchester who has defied my authority. Would you rather I kept him in perpetual imprisonment? Even that would be too great a risk to take."

"The order should not have been given," she said. "It was not done for the city but for your private ends."

I shook my head. "There is no difference."

"You believe that?"

"A Prince must, or he is no Prince."

I put strength into my voice to answer her, but at heart I felt weary, and a dull sickness racked me.

Blodwen said: "What am I in this? A thing? A creature to do her master's bidding, and get a smile from him and perhaps a bauble or two in reward? Are we all things to the Prince of Winchester?"

"I do what has to be done."

"And must we dance to the tune you think you hear? Last night you asked me to swear I did not love Edmund, and I would not do it. Because of that you ordered him on this mission. Did you trust me so little?"

I made no answer. She said:

"We are not puppets, though you would have us so. I do not know what would have happened if you had left well alone. It is no news to me that Edmund loves me, and no surprise that he will defy his Prince for my sake. But I have known his mind better than I knew my own. I would not swear it, not because it was untrue but because I did not know if it were true or not. My father proclaimed our betrothal and I would not willingly thwart his wishes. But I tell you this, Luke: if Edmund is banished then I will go with him and share his exile."

Her words lashed me, with fear as well as pain. In combat I had never known such terror. I looked at her face, unsmiling, lacking any gentleness. I wanted to admit defeat and in doing so beg mercy. I might have still won her if I had. Compassion might not show in her face but it was in her heart always. In defeat I might have conquered.

But I could not trap her with her own pity. I said:

"You may not do it, lady. I am still Prince here, and forbid it."

She smiled then, but with no softening.

"I am not your subject, Luke of Winchester."

"You are in my city."

"My father is Cymru, King of the Wilsh. If I do his bidding it is with consent. No other ruler can bind me."

I felt the fear again, the weakness that was a worse pain than pain. By fighting I must lose everything in the world worth having, and gain nothing. But I could not go back. We faced each other across the narrow room. Behind Blodwen hung the picture of my mother. There, too, was beauty; a beauty which I had worshiped but which had given me small comfort.

I raised my voice: "Guard!"

He clomped in from his post in the Hall of Mirrors. Blodwen still stared at me. I said to the guard:

"The Lady Blodwen is under arrest."

He said impassively: "Yes, sire."

Blodwen said: "Will you throw me in your dungeon?"

Her voice was angry and incredulous. I said:

"Conduct her to her apartments. See that she is well guarded there."

Grimm, the Seer, came to me in mid-morning. He looked as large and easy of mind as ever, but he said:

"Things are in a sorry mess, Luke."

I said: "I have known them better."

"All was going so well." He shook his head. "We must not have an injury to our plans at this stage."

He meant the plans of the High Seers: the plans to restore Science and machines, to transform men's lives. Children's voices called outside as they played some game. The hopes and schemes of the Seers mattered as little to me.

"What do you plan to do with them?" Grimm asked. I did not answer. "Will you hear my advice?"

I said, listening to my own voice's echo and amazed by its seeming calm:

"I will always hear your advice, Grimm."

"Send her back at once to her father's court."

"She will not go without Edmund."

"Then send him with her. Klan Gothlen is far enough away. It is no threat to us."

"And he will have her."

The calmness must have wavered. Grimm stretched his bulky body in the chair. He said:

"Before I became an Acolyte there was a girl from whom I got much misery. Some of our order find it hard to be deprived of women in their lives. I have been glad of it. There are other pleasures."

His belly proved his point. I said:

"I am glad, for your sake."

"Her name was Lucy," Grimm said. "The hurt at that time was great: I thought I would have died of it. But I did not, as you see. And though I remember her name I cannot recall her face. All things pass."

He waited but I said nothing. He said:

"Be careful, Luke. Do nothing rash. Much hangs on you."

I had another visitor: the Christian Bishop. When his name was brought to me, as one requesting audience, I thought of saying no. But any company was better than the company of my thoughts. So I let him in, and looked at him indifferently.

"What do you want?" I asked. "More of my bounty? Have you not had gold and land enough?"

He said: "Men gather in the streets. Only a few so far but the numbers may grow. They cry a name, Prince, but it is not yours. They cry 'Blodwen.' She is well loved by your people."

I laughed. "I have had the Seer telling me what to do but I did not think the Christians would send their Bishop! I did not know you took such interest in the affairs of state."

"Nor do we. I do not speak of politics but of people. One person in particular. She is a good woman."

I stared at him, half angry, half amused.

"That is true, Bishop."

"And honest."

"True also."

"She has done you no wrong." I said nothing to that. "And if you wrong her you will wrong yourself far more."

"I am a Prince," I said. "Remember it."

He shrugged his heavy shoulders and his bald head bobbed.

"That is what they call you. But you are a man first, and she a woman."

"What do you know of men and women? Are you not celibate, to please your god?"

"I know this," he said. "I know that what moves you is not love but pride."

"Of course," I said, "your god called pride a sin. And you cannot be expected to know better. You are not a warrior."

"Whether it be sin or not," he said, "your pride could yet destroy you. Not all your warriors nor your own right arm will save you then."

"You weary me, Bishop," I said. "Go back and pray to your god who had no pride."

• • •

Lastly Jenny came. She had been weeping and her eyes were red still. I said:

"Lady, what service would you do me now?"

"Only to right a wrong."

"No wrong. You called me blind and that was true. My eyes are opened and I thank you."

"There was no truth in it! Edmund did not betray you. I lied in anger." She looked at me, her face a mask of shame. "And in jealousy. I could not bear the way you looked at her. Forgive me, Luke. And do not hold my lies against Edmund." She drew sobbing breath. "Nor against her."

If I had pity to spare I would have pitied her. All that she said was true, and made no difference. I said wearily:

"They love each other. What comes of this must come. There is no profit in regrets."

She turned from me, weeping again, and went away.

I heard the tumult and ran out, my sword bare. The noise came from the north wing, where Blodwen's apartments were. When I got there I found frightened polymufs, splintered doors, one guard dying and one dead. The dying man could not speak and the polymufs were too incoherent to make much sense. There had been fighting, they said, which was plain enough. It was plain also that they had seen nothing because they had hidden out of the way.

But the door to Blodwen's room was smashed, and she was gone.

I was still standing there five minutes later, staring at the broken door, when Greene rode down Sack Street with a dozen of his troop. He dismounted. There was blood on his sleeve but he did not seem badly hurt. I roused myself and said:

"Who took her?"

"Charles."

"*Charles?* How? By himself?"

Because he was Edmund's brother I had that morning, as a precaution, split his troop among other Captains.

Greene said: "He picked up half a dozen of his men. They surprised the guard here. We gave chase but . . ."

"You lost them? It makes no difference. Half a dozen men? He must be mad. And what good does it do to take her? Does he think to use her as a bargain for Edmund's release?"

"He has released Edmund already." I stared at him. "They have the citadel. That was what turned us back."

"Then Blaine . . ." Blaine's men had taken over the citadel guard that morning. "Blaine is with him in this."

Greene nodded. "It seems so."

"So it is rebellion. And Blaine thinks that with his troop and what he can bring together of Charles's, he can take this city?"

"There is more. He has given the Wilsh their swords back. I saw them on the citadel wall."

Disarming Blodwen's Wilsh bodyguard had been another precaution. It was hard to believe that even Blaine could do such a thing as to arm foreign soldiers within the city. But I had no time to waste on incredulity. The revolt was a major one and must be put down. I said to Greene:

"He will be looking for others who may go over to him if they think he is strong enough to win. We need to establish our own strength fast. We must rally those Captains on whom we can rely and get them together, Wilson and Ripon, Nicoll, Barnes, Becket, Stuart."

Greene nodded.

I said: "You go for Nicoll and Barnes. I will get the others. We assemble here, in the palace yard."

• • •

By dusk the lines were drawn. I had failed with Stuart, who had taken his men over to Blaine, and Turner's troop was also in the citadel; but I had expected that. Grant, about whom I had been unsure, on the other hand had stayed loyal. We held the palace and the city in general, they the citadel.

Much hinged on what Harding might do. His troop was perhaps the strongest of all. If they joined us we must win easily: the citadel offered a strong defense but it had never been meant to be impregnable. The city's walls and its warriors had always been our chief safeguard. If he went over to Blaine I was still confident of the outcome, though the fighting would be harder and bloodier.

Harding was no fool; he knew this also. And though he had been no friend of my father or my brother, and was no friend of mine, the hatred between his family and Blaine's went back much further. Nor could I see him joining a rebel who had put arms into the hands of barbarians. He might be treacherous but he loved the city.

The fact that he had not committed himself so far, but kept his troop at that great house of his which was not much smaller than the palace, meant only, I guessed, that he relished the importance of his position. All must see that we waited for him. But he would not put things off too long in case, from impatience, I attacked without him. We could win without his help and that would make him as little as the other made him great.

He came in fact at the hour I expected, and was shown into the hall where I sat with the loyal Captains. He greeted me as a Captain should greet his Prince, the bow brief but unstinted. I said:

"Welcome, Captain! We are glad to have you at our conference. Your counsel will serve us well."

He said: "This is a bad business, sire."

"It is. But can soon be ended."

"Soon maybe, but bitterly. The hatred will not die when the heads of five Captains of Winchester are spiked above the palace gate. The feuds which start today will last for generations."

I said: "This may be so. But we did not start them. What would you have me do?"

"It is said that you were to pronounce banishment on Edmund."

"He refused a command I gave him. Do I not have the right?"

Harding nodded. "You have it. And banishment is better than bloodshed. It might serve better for others, also."

"I am willing to give them exile instead of death. You can take that message to them, if you wish."

"There is a better way. If such a message is sent all must accept or all refuse. They will refuse it therefore. But if we call them to a Captains' conclave, under flag of truce, there is a chance to win them over one by one."

He spoke persuasively, and I saw one or two of our company nod their heads. They were loyal but none was eager for the slaughter of old comrades, in many cases kinfolk. I was not eager for it myself. If it could be settled without bloodshed so much the better. And even if Charles and Edmund and Blaine proved obdurate, Turner and Stuart might not.

I said: "Will they come to such a conclave at the palace, do you think? I will not go to them."

Harding said: "There is my house. It lies between."

We sat in the great hall of Harding's house, at his council table. It was more magnificent than anything

I had in the palace: very long, oval in shape, made of oak that generations of polymuf servants had polished to a dark bloom.

I was at the head, with Greene on my right and the other loyal Captains near. Blaine and his rebels, including Edmund, took the other end of the table. Harding sat in the space between.

We had our swords but were bound in honor not to use them. I did not fear treachery. In any case we outnumbered them and had men within call.

I spoke first and briefly. They were in rebellion against their Prince. It was an act which by law and ancient custom deserved death. This must follow once we had crushed them, and our power to do so was plain.

I offered them their lives, not from weakness but from desire to avoid the spilling of blood. If they surrendered, their men would suffer no penalty. They themselves could take with them into exile whatever movable goods they wished.

Blaine answered me. In Winchester men accepted the rule of Princes but not of tyrants. A Prince might command anything of his Captains but only while his commands served the general welfare. It had not been so in this case. A form of exile had been trumped up against one who had done no wrong, and when it had rightly been rejected banishment had been pronounced. This was tyranny, and it was the duty of citizens to oppose it.

He spoke with his usual bluster. We were all accustomed to it and I did not think anyone was much impressed. In the light of the oil lamps that hung from the ceiling I thought I saw unease in the small eyes, deep set in the fat face.

They would make an offer, he said, in answer to mine. They did not seek bloodshed, either, but peace. If I rescinded the edict of banishment on Edmund and the order of arrest on the lady Blodwen, and restored Charles's troop to him, and promised full amnesty to all, they would come out of the citadel and return to their homes.

It was absurd, of course. After such a confrontation as this there could be no trust. There would be two armies prowling the city, armed and ready to fight at the first provocation. Nor would it be long in coming. And having given way, what authority could I command then? I gave him a blunt refusal, without argument or explanation.

Other Captains spoke. They spoke in accordance with their places at the table, and their temperaments. Some blew hotter and some colder, but the deadlock did not break. Then, when all had had their say, Harding rose to his feet.

I had been waiting for this. His family's nobility was as ancient as Blaine's. He himself had not only served the city well but, unlike fat Blaine, had a reputation for wisdom and sound thinking. When my father was killed it had been Harding who had rallied the Captains. If Peter had not retaken the city there was little doubt he would have been proclaimed Prince. His voice on our side counted for more than all the others put together.

And there was something else. I had spoken to him privately on the way here. Edmund and Charles must go, and Blaine with them, but I had told him that if he asked for pardon for Stuart and Turner I would grant it. They could keep their troops, and even their places in my council. If he put it to them as a duty to the city I was sure they would accept. In this way we would split Blaine's forces; and he himself, seeing his situation as hopeless, would probably choose banishment rather than certain death.

Harding had listened to me, and nodded.

Now he spoke quietly. He spoke of the city, and of the men who had served it through many generations. He did not pick out the deeds of his own family: he did not need to. He spoke of old battles. Victories had united the men of Winchester, but defeats scarcely less. Triumph and disaster had been met together, enjoyed or endured together.

He had their ear. I watched Stuart and Turner, and saw how they were affected. He was leading them with cunning. They would be his men even before he asked for their pardon and I granted it.

But he was in no hurry. He spoke of the increase, in recent years, in the city's power and prosperity. This had happened under the rule of the Perrys. Although not of ancient nobility this family had served the city well: Prince Luke—he bowed slightly to me—not least. When one thought of the city, of its great past and greater future, what did it matter where a girl, even the daughter of a king, bestowed her affections? The Wilsh were a faraway people, and no concern of ours.

I saw Stuart thump the table, and thought: we have them!

Harding paused before he spoke again. He said:

"That is the credit balance. There are also debits to consider. Power and prosperity have grown, but so have discord and intrigue. There has been treachery and plotting and murder, more than was ever known before. And so we come to this moment, with the Captains in arms against each other, the city divided.

"I have said that the affections of a girl do not matter, and that is true. But it involves the Prince, and the Prince involves us all. Can the Prince pardon those who, for any reason, have taken sword against him? And if he does, will not the city fall into new dissension, having a Prince whom none respect?"

He paused once more. "Luke, as Prince, has brought honor to our city. He is a great warrior, though young, and rules not only here but in Petersfield and Romsey as well. But being young he has made mistakes. He burned wheatfields in front of Petersfield, a thing utterly condemned by the Spirits. He made a dwarf warrior, contrary to all custom. And now he has, through passion, brought us to the verge of civil war."

Anger rose in me. There was no mistaking the

change in tone. I knew myself betrayed again and got to my feet. With my hand on my sword hilt, I said:

"Do you challenge me, then, Harding? Does any man?"

Harding shook his head. "I do not challenge you, Luke. There has been enough challenging, enough making and unmaking of Princes. I ask you to do this city a greater service than you have so far done. I ask you to abdicate from ruling."

I laughed. "So that you may peacefully take my place?"

"No." He looked not at me but along the table at the Captains. "Times change. The office of Prince was once a necessary thing, binding the citizens together. But the city has grown and will grow, and it unites us no longer. We are the city, gentlemen, we few. It is we who have the power to rule it, and the responsibility to exercise that power. Today has shown something: that what divides us divides the city. We no longer need one man to tell us what to do. Our wisdom joined together is greater than that of any Prince.

"If one of us challenged Luke and took his place, what good would that do? Would the intrigue and dissension cease? I think they might grow worse. But if power is shared between us there can be an end to envy. What do you think of this?"

The shout of approval from Blaine's end of the table was only to be expected. But I heard others shout with them: Nicoll and Ripon, Becket and Grant and Barnes.

Harding waited until they were quiet; then he said:

"I ask you again, Luke, to do this service. Abdicate peacefully. Join us as a free and equal Captain. You will be welcome in our council."

Their faces swam before me; I was half blind with rage. I said:

"You know your answer."

"Then I must put another proposition to the assembly," Harding said. "That we dismiss this Prince, doing him no hurt, and exile him from our city. Raise your right hands, all who approve of it."

Their hands went up: Blaine's, Edmund's, Charles's, Stuart's and Turner's. And with them Nicoll's, Ripon's, Becket's, Grant's, Barnes's. At last, slowly, without looking at me, Greene raised his hand with the rest. Only old Wilson sat unmoving.

"The majority favors it," Harding said. "We rest the authority of Winchester in the council of Captains."

I said: "I claim the right of any Prince to challenge his usurper! Or will you make an end of honor?"

"There is no usurper, Captain Perry," Harding said. "And the word Prince has lost its meaning. Leave us, and go in peace into your exile."

I half-drew my sword. Their eyes watched me, my enemies and my false friends. There were enough who would be glad of the excuse to cut me down. I let the sword slip back.

"This is not the end," I said. "I am your Prince still, and the day will come when you know it. Remember today's work well. There will be a bloody harvest from this sowing."

Harding smiled. "Go in peace, while you still may."

I turned and left them.

SIX

A WEAPON FROM THE PAST

I SAW ANOTHER DAWN BREAK NEXT DAY, FOR I left the city while it was still dark. I would not stay for daylight and accept the shame of pointing fingers and the jeers of the mob. And revenge spurred me on equally with shame. The sooner I was away, the sooner I could return. Harding's head, I vowed, would sit above those of the rest.

While I was in the stables, saddling my horse, I heard a sound from the shadows behind me. I turned swiftly, hand on sword. It was not impossible, not even unlikely, that for all the talk of doing me no hurt, an assassin or more than one had been put to seek me out and kill me. Both Blaine and Harding were capable of it.

But the figure spoke as it came forward. "It is I, sire." I recognized the dwarfish frame. It was Hans.

I said: "How did you know I would be here?"

"I did not," Hans said, "but I knew you would need your horse. I was waiting until you came."

"All night?"

He shrugged. "I dozed. We dwarfs are easy sleepers."

I took his hand. "It was a kind thought, to bid me good-by. I am glad of it."

"Not that, sire. I come to travel with you."

"No. That too warms me. But the journey I go I must make alone. Return to your home, Hans."

He said quietly, in his deep rasping voice:

"I have no home here now."

I recalled what he had said a moment before: "we dwarfs." He had left Dwarftown to serve me as a warrior. That was something which could not survive my going. He had lost everything as I had done, and it mattered as much to him as it did to me.

"Then come with me," I said. I laughed. "The High Seers must take us both together."

"The High Seers?" He was startled. "You go to Sanctuary, sire?"

Dwarfs did not pay much attention to the Spirits, but it was a dread thought to envisage going to the place men said was their stronghold. I said:

"You need not go there if you fear it. We will find a place where you can wait for me. In Salisbury, perhaps."

"I will go where you go, sire. I do not fear it."

"Good!" I said. "But no 'sires,' Hans. 'Sire' is for Princes and I am Prince no longer. You may call me Captain: they have left me that."

Hans shook his head. "You are Prince to me, sire. And always will be."

It was strange that the loyalty of a single man, a dwarf, could mean more than a city's acclamation. I turned my face away.

"Saddle yourself a horse, Hans," I said. "Take which you will. All are sound beasts. This was the Prince's stable."

We spent that night at the court of Prince Matthew of Andover.

The last time I had been his guest had been on

my journey south with Ezzard, after Peter called me back from Sanctuary. But we had met more recently, when he came to Winchester for the ball in Blodwen's honor. I had had much flattery from him then.

He was a stupid amiable man, with a thin dull face and scanty reddish hair. His chief concern, as far as one could see, was ceremony. The army of Andover might not do conspicuously well in battle, but no other city's troops could match them in turn-out and parade drill. The guard that saluted us at the gate wore a breastplate that he must have sat up all night polishing.

The pigeons, I knew, would have brought news of what had happened in Winchester. People gathered in small knots as we rode through the streets, silent and curious. At the palace—not a large building but freshly painted in stripes of black and white—we dismounted, and I left Hans with the horses. I was admitted to Matthew's council chamber, and he wasted no time in making the position clear.

He remained seated as I crossed the room toward him. I bowed and said:

"Greetings, sire."

He did not return the bow. With a stiff face, he said:

"Greetings, Captain Perry."

But once he had established what we two were—himself a Prince and I a landless wanderer—he could permit some amiability to show again. He ordered a room to be prepared for me in the palace, and bade me join him that evening at his table. And I mustered the grace somehow to thank him for his hospitality.

I told myself that I could spurn no possible ally, even this fool with his passion for putting things neatly in rows. At supper that night I talked of what had happened. This embarrassed him but he offered cold sympathy. I led him to the point I wished to make, putting it broadly enough to penetrate his narrow skull but delicately as befitted one who was no longer a royal cousin but a vagabond. The point was this: if one city could unmake its Prince and replace him by a council of Captains, others might do likewise.

He took it but was not impressed. From stupidity again, I thought, and lack of imagination, but I misjudged him there. He said, with more cunning than I would have given him credit for:

"Who proposed your deposition in that council? Harding. So at the outset he speaks for the others. It is a council of Captains but one man is its voice. How long before he has a Prince's power, and once he has that will he not take the name?"

It was something that had occurred to me also. Blaine would fight him to the end, but Blaine was no match for him in craft. Nor would Blaine's arming of the Wilsh be soon forgotten.

I said: "This may be. But if such a pretext can be used once it can be used again. It sets the authority of Captains above that of Prince."

"I do not think so, Perry." My own name was an insult. He smiled complacently. "I am safe from challenge from my Captains."

"As short a time since as yesterday morning, I thought the same."

Impatience and anger had sharpened my voice. He frowned at that. There were tones to use to Princes, and this was not among them. His own voice turned hard.

"But I am not likely to lose my head over a wench," he said.

He stared at me, weak blue eyes narrowed in a spite that must always have lain hidden behind the flattery he showed me at my court.

"Nor burn harvest crops. Nor call a dwarf warrior, offending warriors of true human stock. Nor take another Prince's city as my own."

He watched me. Anger burned my mind, forging bitter words to answer him. But I held them back. I had offended him already. Offending him further might well be enough to earn me a place in his cells. And once in them, the Great alone knew when I would be freed.

So I said: "You are right, sire. I am punished for my faults."

His smile returned. He clapped his hands and a polymuf brought another dish to the table.

"Try this meat, Perry. We have done well for boar this year."

I was shivering. "I am not hungry, sire."

Matthew leaned forward. "But I would have you eat."

There was no ally here but a Prince I must obey. I took meat and forced myself to eat it.

. . .

Tired though I was I had little sleep that night. My thoughts were baying hounds that leaped round me, their stricken prey, savage and merciless. I tried to kill them, but from each blow they rose and gave louder tongue. And the hounds wore mocking faces: Harding, Blaine, Greene. Most of all, Edmund and Blodwen. They laughed at me and at each other; but the first was the laughter of scorn, the second of joy and desire.

And with this I sweated and shivered. In the morning my limbs were heavy and my head ached with a pain that throbbed behind my eyes. The shivering would not stop. Matthew noticed it when I went to pay my respects on departure. He asked:

"Are you well, Perry?"

"Well enough, sire."

"You do not look well. You are welcome to stay longer, and I can have my surgeon sent to you. Or at least one of his assistants."

I gritted my teeth. My need to be clear of this man and his court put aside for a moment my other thoughts of hatred and revenge. I said:

"I am very well, sire. I will not trespass further on your kindness."

Hans when he saw me was alarmed. He too urged me to stay in Andover, at an inn if not at the palace. We had enough gold to pay for a lodging. But I would not listen to him; I had to be out in the open.

He said: "Do we make for Salisbury now, sire?"

We had gone north, out of our direct way, to avoid Romsey land. I did not know what resentments lingered there and might be exercised against one who had conquered them as Prince but now was powerless.

"We ride that way," I said, "but we will not enter the city." He looked at me. "While I lack power I will stay away from cities."

"And in Sanctuary the Spirits will give you power?"

My head was light and heavy at the same time. I laughed.

"If they do not, I think no one else will!"

We were riding down the main street that led from the palace. Three black-robed figures walked the opposite way: the Seer of Andover with two Acolytes. He saw me but affected not to know me, and I rode past with no salute. The Seers could do nothing for me at this point; and to have commerce with me would compromise them needlessly. Ezzard's fate was still remembered. It was because of this that I had left Winchester without seeing Grimm.

I rode on to the West Gate. My head throbbed with pain and anger. The Seers could do nothing for me. The High Seers in Sanctuary were a different matter.

The day was windless but the cold bit savagely and deep into the bone. The sky was dark gray with a shade of pink in it: full of snow. Some was shed during the morning. Small flakes, scarcely more than white dust, floated slow, slow, and specked the frozen ground. By midday the snow had stopped, but the sky above us looked ready to burst with it.

We stopped to eat at an inn high up in the hills. I had no hunger but forced myself to take something; not this time to suit another's whim but to keep up my strength. I knew now I had a fever. My forehead burned when I put up a hand to wipe it. I saw my Aunt Mary again, and heard her say: "Starve a fever, child . . ." All right for a child at home, I told her, tucked in a warm cot—a journey in this weather was a different matter. Hans said: "Sire?" and I realized I must have mumbled words aloud. "Nothing,"

I told him, and returned to my dish. It was a game pie, foul looking and foul tasting. I felt sick but chewed and swallowed as best I could.

We rode again, and the snow came down more thickly. The flakes were bigger and began to whirl in dance as the wind got up.

Hans pointed. "Is that not Amesbury, sire?" I nodded. "It might be best to take shelter there. It will be worse before long."

"No." I heard my voice buzz and echo. "We will pass to the south of it. We can reach Sanctuary by nightfall."

We came to the river and had to go south again, a long way south, to find a ford. The snow played a game with us, almost stopping and then blowing fierce in our faces. I felt giddy. My head at one moment was a bladder, which I feared might float off my shoulders and away among the snowflakes; the next a lump of aching lead.

I had been a fool not to do as Hans said. Snow covered the country all round us, obliterating landmarks. A fool in this, and in so many other things. Prince of Three Cities but two days since, and now . . . My teeth chattered in my burning head.

Then the chattering and the burning and even the pain seemed to go far away, out into the flickering whiteness of the sky.

Hans cried: "Sire, are you all right?"

I could not answer him. I felt myself slipping from the saddle and tried to grip the rein, but my hand would not obey me. The whiteness all round turned to black.

The nightmare had many parts to it and many characters. Harding was there and I cursed him. I swore vengeance, and saw the vengeance taken. His head stared down from the palace gate and a crow plucked his eyes. Then that changed, and it was not the palace gate but the East Gate, and the head was my father's. I wept, and beside me Harding laughed. Then in fury I killed him again and butchered his body with my steel. And the bleeding corpse got up, and mocked me still.

Edmund was there, too. I rode with him by the Contest Field, and pleaded with him, for our friendship's sake, not to wrong me. He spoke me fair, but looked beyond me and smiled at someone else. I knew who it was that won a smile he had never given me.

Blodwen came to me alone. She stood on the stair above her father's throne room, and said: "I will be my own woman always. Remember that, Luke of Winchester. I will be my own woman." "Be what you will," I cried, "as long as you are mine!" "I will be my own woman, Luke of Winchester . . ." "Be that, but not his, not his . . ." She smiled, and I cried: "Swear you do not love him!" She shook her lovely head. "No. That I will not swear." "You are mine! Mine, and I shall have you." She shook her head again. "No. You never will. But it does not matter. It does not matter because you are dying, Luke, in the snow. Edmund has me, and you are dying, dying . . ."

Then it was over. My spirit floated in air, without substance, without organs, but I saw and heard. She and Edmund walked together in the palace garden, their fingers linked. They whispered and I heard their whispering. "Poor Luke, dead in the snow. Poor Luke." They laughed and, laughing, kissed.

My spirit winged like a bird, high over the city walls and across the blind white land. I hunted for my body, with one end in view. A body had an arm and an arm could hold a sword, and a sword would cut them down . . .

All this and more. Time had no meaning, any more than place or person. It went on endlessly, the taking and giving of pain. But at last there was quiet, and after the quiet, voices that neither jeered nor wept, but spoke evenly and with sense. I knew the voices, and knew this was no dream. I opened my eyes and there was whiteness here, too, but the whiteness of sheet and pillowslip. And I saw the broad wrinkled face of Murphy, the High Seer, clear in electric light.

He smiled. "How are you, Luke?"

"Well enough." I felt weak but the fever was gone. "How did I get here?"

"You have that dwarf of yours to thank."

"Hans? Is he well?"

"Yes. Since you were here last we have set up a television scanner on one of the standing stones. The barbarians press closer from the west all the time, and we cannot be sure they will recognize holy ground when they see it. We need to keep an eye open for visitors. But scarcely in a blizzard. Robb switched it on to make the routine test we carry out once a day. And to his astonishment he saw two horses coming up the hill through the snowstorm, with a dwarf mounted on one and a body strapped to the other. And as they neared the circle the snow cleared and he saw the body had a face he knew."

"Hans brought me here? That took courage."

"So I would think." Murphy chuckled. "You should have seen his face when the earth opened up in front of him!"

I thought of it. To have followed me to Sanctuary would have been a great enough thing. I remembered my own fear when I first saw the Stones, enormous in the empty hillside, and that had been on a fair day, with Ezzard the Seer guiding me. To have ridden up into the dread circle through a snowstorm, leading my horse with me unconscious or even dead on its back . . . I had been right to make him warrior. I did not think there was another in my army who could have done it.

My army . . . I said:

"He has told you what happened—or what he knows of it?"

"We knew already," Murphy said. "From Grimm."

Of course. Pigeons might not fly in a blizzard, but nothing stopped the invisible radio waves which bound the Seers in the cities to the High Seers in Sanctuary.

"I have served you and your cause," I said. "Now I come to you for help."

"You were right to do so."

"I want . . ."

I started to rise from the bed but weakness made me fall back. Murphy said:

"There will be plenty of time to talk of what you want. Get your strength back first."

"Is Hans . . . ?"

"We had difficulty in getting him from your bedside but in the end tiredness overcame him. He is sleeping. You need to do the same."

It was two days later—days marked by electric clocks, not by the rising and setting of the sun—that I spoke to the High Seers together. We sat in the big room whose walls were painted with landscapes, a trick to deceive the mind into thinking we were not underground but looking out through windows at the living earth. I do not know about the High Seers but my mind was not deceived. It made me miss the reality all the more.

But the High Seers, perhaps, having lived in this way so long, had grown used to it. And they had their mission, compared with which nothing else mattered. I looked at them: Lanark, Murphy, Robb, Gunter and the rest. They wore no formal robes but ordinary simple clothes, and their heads were not cropped. There was nothing to remark on in them. Nothing except the knowledge they held and hoped to restore; and the power that knowledge gave.

They put questions to me and I answered them as patiently as I could. Murphy said:

"It is a setback. There is no denying it. But there are favorable possibilities. This Eric of Oxford, who favors change. He is only Prince in Waiting, but we may be able to do something about that. Lukis is Seer in Oxford . . ."

I interrupted him. "I am sure there are intrigues that can be woven. But I did not come for this."

Murphy started to speak again but old Lanark put a hand up to stop him. He said:

"Let Luke speak."

I tapped the sword in my belt. There was no need for it here but I wore it. Perhaps it did for me what the painted walls did for the High Seers. What tricks the mind is what the mind is glad to be tricked by.

"You gave me this," I said, "the Sword of the Spirits. I killed my brother with it and took the city which you had planned I should have. But the city is lost to us now, and no sword will win it back. I need another weapon."

They were silent, watching me.

"Our ancestors had weapons which killed at a distance. They called them firearms. You know of them and can make them for me."

Robb said: "You would still need an army. One man cannot conquer a city even with firearms."

"I will get an army."

"From Oxford?" Murphy said. He shook his head. "Even if Eric were Prince he could not put guns in the hands of his army. There more than in most places their minds are closed against such things, but there is not a city throughout the civilized lands where men would accept them."

"Not in the civilized lands," I said, "but there is a city. The Prince at night watches a cinematograph film. They cut grass with machines and have crossbows to drive arrows. His Chancellor is polymuf."

"Klan Gothlen? It lies very far away. And what

makes you think that Prince would help you? His daughter is in Winchester, and your enemy."

"He owes me a debt."

"Debts are not always paid."

"One can seek payment."

Murphy shrugged, in doubt. But Lanark said:

"This may offer something. There is no harm in trying in that quarter as well as at Oxford. We could send someone north in the spring, and see how the land lies."

"The weapon," I said. "You could give me such a thing?"

Lanark said to Robb: "Do you have a film to show us?"

"I think I can find what you want."

While he was getting the film and others set up screen and projector, I said to Lanark:

"I thought I might find Martin here. He arrived safely?"

Lanark nodded. "And went on."

"Went on? Where?"

"To the other Sanctuary. In the ruins of London."

"You sent him there?"

"No. It was his choice."

"What is it he is seeking?"

"I do not know," Lanark said, "but he did not find it here."

Robb ran the film. It was not like that scratched and jerky picture of comic animals which I had seen at Cymru's court. What one saw, unlike the paintings on the wall, looked almost real enough to touch. Men walked across a field, a line of fifty or more of them. They walked easily, talking and laughing. Then one saw other men, a few only, waiting in a thicket at the field's end. They carried long tubes of metal, with a triangle at the end and something sticking down underneath. They raised the triangles to their shoulders and put their hands round the part beneath. Harsh and savage sound, the stammering of tongueless giants, broke out. And the line of men fell, sinking like wheat to the sickle's sweep.

Robb switched off the projector and put up the room lights. He said:

"Is that the sort of thing you want?"

I was amazed and shocked, but I said: "Yes. And they can be made? Not just one, but many?"

Robb was a short thin man, with a skin even more pallid than the other High Seers. He wore spectacles with lenses of thick glass. He said:

"Many of our ancestors' weapons were complex things, but this is not. They called it the Sten gun. It can be made fairly easily."

"Can it be used on horseback?"

"Probably. But a man on foot would control it better."

Lanark said: "You say the sword we gave you is no longer enough, Luke, that you need a far more powerful weapon. You may be right. But you must understand that other changes follow the changes of weapons. Horses are bigger targets against guns than men on foot. When the Sten gun returns there will be no more riding into battle."

I nodded, scarcely listening, seeing my enemies—Harding, Blaine, Edmund and the rest—struck down in their triumph and laughter.

"There is another thing," Lanark said. "You are a man of Winchester. You found it hard to believe that Blaine could put swords into the hands of the Wilsh to fight his own people. Will you take a whole army of Wilsh against your city, and with weapons such as these? Do you think you can?"

I saw the council of Captains with their hands raised against me. And I remembered Edmund and Blodwen in the dream, whispering, laughing, kissing.

I said: "Have no fear, Lanark. I will do it."

SEVEN

THE PEOPLE OF THE BELLS

HANS, AFTER THE FIRST SHOCK, ACCUS-tomed himself well to life in Sanctuary and to the wonders the High Seers showed him. He watched them at work in the laboratories, and put questions which they answered. Apart from the power it might give, this science of theirs had small interest to me. It was not so with Hans. Although his chief passion had been to serve as a warrior, rather than be an armorer like his father, he came of a long line of metal-working craftsmen. Once he had accepted the idea of machines he saw easily enough how they worked. The High Seers were ready to instruct him, and he was quick to learn.

Robb and a man called Kinnell were the ones principally concerned with the Sten gun. I listened when Hans spoke to them but made little sense of it. There was talk of cordite, of percussion caps, of blow-back open-bolt action—and a dozen other things which to me meant nothing. All I was aware of was the gun itself taking shape. I gazed at it as a hungry man might watch a rabbit roasting, tantalized and impatient.

At last it was finished and we gathered in one of the storerooms to see it work. A target was set up at the far end. Robb showed me how to hold the gun and press the trigger. I lifted it and fired. I felt it jerk, almost like a living thing, and the noise of the tongueless stammering giant echoed in the room. And the target showed a ragged line of holes.

Until now, despite the ancient film they had shown me, I had not really believed in the power of this weapon. But it was no longer possible to doubt. I lowered the gun and said:

"You have done well, Robb."

"It is not so accurate as other weapons of the

past," he said. "And the range is no more than about two hundred yards."

"Two hundred yards is enough. Give me a hundred of them, fifty even, and no army will stand against me."

Robb laughed. "We chose this gun because it was the simplest to make, but it still needs making! And we have no more than two hands apiece. Fifty, you say? By next autumn, perhaps, but I would not guarantee it."

"Autumn! I need them long before that."

"You are impatient, Luke," Lanark said, "and we understand why. But things must take their time. It is not only a question of guns. You have an army to find as well. We must wait till winter ends before we can sound out the Wilsh King. And then our messenger will need to go about it warily."

"It is I who must ask it of Cymru."

"And chance being sent back to Winchester with your hands roped behind you? Or maybe executed on the spot for the insult to his daughter? It would be an absurd risk to take. No, Luke, this is something you must leave to us."

I spoke to Hans next morning when he came to clean my room.

The High Seers had no servants, except for the machines invented by our ancestors to ease house labor. Each looked after himself, even old Lanark. But Hans would have none of this. It was not proper, he said, for a Prince to do such things. The High Seers laughed, but Hans paid no heed and continued to serve me. And I accepted the service, knowing that to reject it would be an insult.

So I watched while he used the machine that cleaned the floor, sucking up dirt and dust. It made a whining noise as it moved, a scream of protest such as one would never have heard from a polymuf. At last he switched it off and it was possible to speak. And for once we were alone with none to hear what passed between us.

I said: "This Sten gun, Hans—you have watched the making and listened to what Robb and Kinnell said of it?"

"Yes, sire."

"And understood?" He nodded. "You could make such a thing yourself? The bullets also? And teach others to do the same?"

"Yes. It would not be difficult, as long as one could get the materials. For cordite one needs gun cotton and nitroglycerine. Gun cotton itself requires sulphuric and nitric acids . . ."

I cut him short. "It means nothing to me. What matters is that it does to you. The Wilsh would have these things? Or could get them?"

"Yes. It would be no more difficult than making the asbestos cloth, out of chrysotile, which the peddler used to cross the Burning Lands."

"And therefore their craftsmen could make these Sten guns?"

"Yes." He nodded. "Even though most of them are not dwarfs, they do not lack skill."

"Good! That is what I hoped to hear. Hans, I think it is time we went on another journey."

"To Klan Gothlen? But the High Seers forbid it."

"They had me penned in once before," I said, "for the greater part of a winter. But I was a boy then. I did not come here to be treated like a boy again."

"Sire," he said earnestly, "hear me. There is wisdom in what they say. If you go to Cymru, he may imprison or even kill you. They are a strange people,

the Wilsh. They smile easily, but they are good haters too. And the lady Blodwen meant much to them."

"I will take that chance."

"And it is high winter. And we have no horses.
Those on which we came were sent to the Seer's
stable at Amesbury."

All this was true and made sense. Few traveled in
the winter, and then no farther than to the next city.
Earlier that morning I had looked through the television scanner and seen nothing but a white whirling
wilderness. It made no difference. I said:

"Will you come with me, Hans, if I ask it?"

He looked at me. "You know it, sire."

The blizzard raged two days more. The morning
after the snow stopped we left Sanctuary before anyone else was stirring. I pressed the button on the top
landing of the staircase and the trap door opened
over our heads, creaking more than usual under its
weight of snow. Some of the snow scattered down
on us. It brought with it the cold sting of fresh air
and I drew deep breath to fill my lungs.

During those two days, taking care not to be
observed, Hans had packed rucksacks for us, with
food and other things we would need on the journey.

He had also made us snowshoes, such as peasants wear to cross their fields in winter, using plastic instead of the usual strips of hide in a wooden frame. They were oval in shape, about a foot long, and had straps that buckled over our boots.

Even so the going was hard. I was not used to walking; even to go from the palace to the River Road I would have taken horse. And although the shoes prevented one's feet from sinking below the surface, the snow dragged at them. It was not long before the muscles at the backs of my legs were aching from the strain, and within an hour I had to call a halt to rest. Hans fared better: a dwarf is more strongly muscled in the leg and he had used his more.

I had forgotten also how much wider the world is to a man on foot than it is to a horseman. One would see a mark in the distance and reckon ten minutes as the time needed to reach it. Half an hour later it would seem scarcely nearer. The monotony of the trudging was worse than the fatigue; my muscles accustomed themselves to the strain sooner than my mind did.

We were nearly three days getting to the pass that

crossed the Burning Lands. We avoided towns and villages, where travelers at this season would excite interest, but did stay one night at an isolated farm. I told a story of a pilgrimage imposed by the Seer on account of an unwitting act of impiety toward the Spirits. They accepted this but expressed surprise that a dwarf should be my servant. Hans accounted for it by telling them he was not dwarf but polymuf, with marks on his body beneath his clothes. It must have cost him dearly in pride to do so.

The second night we found a deserted hut and slept there. And in the afternoon of the third day we came to the dead landscape lying under the hills of the Burning Lands, where snow gave way to black rock and steaming pools. We took off our snow-shoes and started on the last mile or two leading to the pass.

I had thought winter might have chilled the black sand underfoot and made our crossing easier, but it seemed to have had no effect on it. We had each brought three extra pairs of boots, changing them as they got too hot, but we scorched our feet all the same. We crossed, however, and soaked our legs in a tepid pool while our last pairs of boots cooled off.

They had suffered badly; and we still had something like two hundred miles of rough and wintry country to travel.

At least it no longer mattered who saw us. We found a village before nightfall, a primitive place but with a cobbler who, for gold, sat up all night and had new boots ready for us in the morning. Hans shook his head over the workmanship—they were poor objects by our Winchester standards—but they would serve.

So we went north, taking much the same route as we had taken under Greene's command when the peddler guided us. But that had been in spring and on horseback. Now we plodded over fields of snow, wearily through a barren world. We saw few animals, rabbits or an occasional hare, its ears pricked in silhouette against the white skyline, slinking foxes, ermine, once a wild boar. I would have welcomed a change from the dried meat we had brought with us. Given a horse and spear I could have run it down easily. I thought of the Sten gun, which would have killed it more easily still, and put my hand to where it hung at my belt. But though we had brought several magazines of bullets, I would not use it. We must make do with the rations we had.

At last we reached the river whose valley we had followed before. Fresh blizzards sprang up soon after, but we found shelter in a village. We stayed two days, in a stinking hut with stinking savages, taking turns to sleep at night in case one of them seized an opportunity to cut our throats. Though I doubt if there was any real danger of it. They were a cowed lot, undernourished and of poor physique, and they seemed to regard us with fear. All the same I was glad when we could go on.

The river was frozen and there were marks on the fresh snow that covered it, showing where animals had crossed. Some of the prints were very large, much bigger than those of a man, and made, I realized when I studied them, by some creature that walked upright as a man does. Whatever it may have been, we did not see it.

Although the snow had stopped, the wind remained strong and a little west of north. It blew in our faces on the valley floor and we went up onto higher ground where pine trees covering the ridge offered some protection. It was from these trees, in mid-afternoon, that the attack came.

I was not looking that way and my first awareness arose from Hans' cry of alarm. We were some ten yards apart—he had stopped to tighten a strap on his snowshoes while I plodded on—and I looked back to see long dark shapes racing down the slope toward him. I barely had time to recognize them as huge dogs, a dozen or more, before they reached him. The leader leaped in a great arc, covering many feet of intervening space. Hans put up his arms in defense, but the beast's weight smashed him to the ground.

Others were on him as he fell. They had swept down from the trees in silence but now they gave savage tongue. Half of them were mauling Hans and the rest ran on toward me. I lifted the Sten gun, not bothering to aim, and fired at them. One fell; at once the others turned tail.

Those attacking Hans retreated also. I went to him and helped him to rise. He was bleeding heavily from bites on the arms, which he had used to protect his face and throat from their teeth. I let go my support of him and he moaned and fell. I saw then that blood was also gushing from his right leg.

I tore up a linen shirt from my pack and set to

work to bind up the wounds. That in the leg was the ugliest, a long tear exposing bloody muscle and sinew. It was plain that, tough as he was, he would not be able to stand, let alone walk.

I looked up the snow slope to the line of trees. Shapes skulked there, watchful. One howled, and others followed suit. Their presence being known, there was no need for silence.

We had been told of these creatures by the peddler. They were polyhounds who hunted in packs and, like the building rats, showed signs of more intelligence than a beast should have. A troop of horse such as we then were would be unlikely to encounter them, the peddler said. They watched for people traveling alone or in small groups.

Probably they had been silently tracking us for some time, and had attacked when they could surprise us separated from one another. It was a further indication, both of their cunning and their ferocity, that although the Sten gun had caused an immediate retreat they had not gone far.

They were still much too near for comfort. I got Hans to take a hold round my neck and staggered, carrying him on my back, down toward the valley floor. When we had covered twenty or thirty yards, he said:

"They are coming after us."

I set him down and fired at them again, and again they retreated into the line of trees. This happened several times, and I scored a hit on one of them at least; it limped away howling and dripping blood on the snow. But the time came when they did not go back as far as the trees. Instead they moved out and round, making a great circle which had us as its center. I tasted fear in my throat, understanding what had happened: by trial and error they had estimated the Sten gun's range and taken up positions outside it.

The valley was white and empty, apart from us and the surrounding polyhounds. From time to time there were bursts of howling; but their silences were more chilling still. I remembered something else the peddler had said: although hunger might sometimes drive them to attack by day, they were reckoned far more dangerous by night. Already the afternoon was fading into dusk.

I carried Hans, and rested, and carried him again. The polyhounds kept pace and distance, moving when we moved and stopping when we stopped.

Progress was arduous, and painfully slow. Hans said at last:

"Sire, you must leave me and go on."

We had covered scarcely a quarter of a mile. I said, panting:

"It is true, I might find help. There was a village where the river forked—do you remember? It cannot be more than a few miles north. I could bring men back with me."

Hans looked up from where he crouched in the snow.

"Yes. I will be all right till then."

I handed him the gun. He tried to refuse it, but I said:

"They know we can wound or kill them from a distance. Therefore they will keep clear of both of us while it is light. But after that you may need to hold them off for a time. I will return as quickly as I can."

I set off before he could make further protest. The polyhounds also moved. Half followed me while the rest kept their places around Hans. I went a hundred yards, a hundred and fifty. Then Hans' voice came to me, urgently shouting:

"Back, sire! Come back!"

I had already seen it: the ones that had followed me were closing in. They moved to head me off as I doubled back. I saw one brute loping in toward me and cursed the hampering snowshoes I wore, though I would have been little better off without them. He must intercept me. But the Sten gun chattered and he dropped with a scream of pain. The others fell away and I reached Hans.

It took me some moments to gather breath to speak.

"Cunning indeed," I said. "They know there is only one gun, and saw me give it to you."

"You must take it," Hans said. "And you must go on. The gun is only of use while there is light. After that, nothing will stop them."

The polyhounds had taken up the same circle as before, just out of range. I said:

"I will get some of them, even in the dark."

"But it serves no purpose, sire. Remember, you have a mission."

A mission? He meant, of course, the task laid on me by the High Seers. As if that mattered compared with the life of someone who had twice saved mine. But there was something else, deep in the darkness of my mind. Hans was right in saying that I could not save him by staying: I would only lose my own life along with his. Yet it was not that which filled me with despair and bitterness. It was the thought of dying with my revenge unaccomplished.

I think he read uncertainty in my face. He said:

"Go, sire. You must do your duty as a Prince. Nothing else matters."

I had left him before in the hope of bringing back help. There was nothing like this now; they would be on him, tearing him to pieces, as soon as I was gone. I shook my head, to clear the black madness from it. I said harshly:

"I am staying, Hans. That is a Prince's duty; and a friend's."

I looked past him to the polyhounds. They had ceased their howling and were silent. They seemed to be listening to something. There was no sound but that of our breathing and the wind's distant sighing in the pines. Or was there a noise, faint and far off? I strained my ears and heard it. Scarcely audible, it rose and fell with the gusting wind: a tiny jangling tinkle of bells.

The polyhounds had heard it, too. They barked,

one to another like men in council. Then the circle was broken as they ran round us to re-form their pack on the slope above. They ran, silent again, into the cover of trees and disappeared.

I saw figures come into view, bearing down the slope from the north, below the tree line. They were men, but traveling so fast over the snow that I wondered if some sort of machine carried them. But as they came nearer I saw that they were sliding on long thin planks. I waved and shouted and they changed course, dipping down the valley's side toward us.

They were more than a score in number. They were dressed in furs and looked strong and healthy, well nourished. They greeted us amiably and asked what help we needed.

I told them of the polyhounds and they nodded. They often warred with these beasts and had their measure. One of them, smiling, tapped a wicked-looking knife in his belt and showed a fur cap with half a dozen polyhound tails dangling from it.

They had ropes, and made a litter to carry Hans. Some went on down the valley, moving fast on the thin planks which they called skis, but the rest accompanied us at our slower pace. We traveled south a couple of miles; then west up a side valley. Their village was there. The huts were stoutly built of wood. Blue smoke rose from chimneys and there was an appetizing smell of food cooking.

People came out to greet us. These too were healthy and had smiling faces. The women took Hans and saw to his wounds, replacing my rough bandages with others of clean linen, smeared with a healing ointment. Others poured hot spiced ale into pots for the returning hunters, and for me also.

Unlike that other village in which we had stayed, this one was pleasant, and so were its inhabitants. There were many items one could note: the stoutness and cleanliness of the huts, the signs of good husbandry and prosperity—bins brimming with fat corn, smoked hams and sides of salmon hanging from the roof beams—the comeliness of both men and women, the vigor and merriness of the children. But I felt there was more to it than the sum of these parts. There was a sense of warmth and ease which went deep. It was not quite like anything I had known.

I was concerned at first about their reaction to

the Sten gun. Either they might, as would have been the case in the lands of the south, regard it as an evil thing and Hans and me as deserving of death for possessing it; or they might covet it for its power. But neither was the case. They looked at it with scarcely even curiosity, and no desire for possession.

They were altogether strangely incurious. I told them, in explanation of how we got there, that we came from the south and were traveling to Klan Gothlen and the court of King Cymru. They nodded, indicating that they had heard of the city and the king, but asked no other questions.

It was plain that we must stay with them for some days, while Hans' wounds healed. I offered gold for our lodging. They glanced at the coins with as little interest as they had shown in the Sten gun, and handed them back. Hospitality needed no payment. They might have added, but did not, that in any case they had no use for gold.

During the days that followed I came to know them, and their way of life, better. There was one man, older and bigger than the rest, to whom—it seemed to me—some deference was paid. I guessed he was their chief, and addressed him as such. He denied it, smiling. His name was Jok, and he had no title. None of them did. They had heard of kings and chiefs and such, but there was none here.

I did not believe him at first, thinking it some pretense of modesty or custom. I asked who made decisions among them. He said the Tribe did. But what, I asked, if the Tribe were divided among itself? Jok laughed. That could not be! One might as well speak of a man's left arm being divided from his right.

This did not convince me. I did not see how any group of people could live together without dissension, always in agreement. It made no sense. But as time passed, though I looked for discord among them, I found none.

They had no marriage as such, and no paternity. The children were children of the Tribe, not of a particular couple. They called all women Mother, all men Father. In a similar fashion those of adult years, when they did not use given names, called each other Brother and Sister.

Most of the things they did seemed to follow one person's prompting, the rest falling in with whatever notion was put forward. Nor was it always the same person, or group of people, who suggested things. It was almost as though they thought with a single mind, so that it did not matter whose voice it was first uttered any project.

The men were hunters; the women cooked and cleaned for them and cared for the sick and old and, of course, the children. In summer, men and women worked together in the fields, sharing the labor of sowing and planting and harvesting. I saw there were no polymufs or dwarfs among them, and asked about that. I was told they were smothered at birth. This was not out of revulsion or in obedience to the behest of Spirits, but from kindness. It would be cruel, they felt, to let a crippled child live, different from his brothers and sisters and deprived of the fullness of activity which they enjoyed.

And what, I asked, if a man or woman were crippled later in life: in the hunt, perhaps? Again it was Jok I was talking to, and he shook his head. Such a person would be well cared for, in hope of recovery. Should the time come when he knew he would not regain his true strength, he would bid farewell to the Tribe and leave the village. There was an herb growing in the woods which brought a quiet death.

The whole village was a place of cheerful noise. They talked and laughed much, and apart from that there were the bells. They had a passion for them. They wore small bells on their clothes, and larger ones hung outside the huts, to jangle with each puff of wind, and inside on intricate arrangements of cords which could be agitated by the touch of a hand or even by the chance pressure of a footstep. They were so delicately balanced that they would go on sounding long afterward.

Hans' wounds healed fast: perhaps because of the ointment the women put on them and perhaps to some extent through the happiness and contentment we found here. I had often heard it said that a wound stays angry where a warrior has an angry wife. It may be the opposite is true also.

The days passed easily. I practiced wearing these skis of theirs and in due course went out with the men to hunt, following clumsily and falling a lot in the snow but managing on the whole to keep up with them. We killed deer and boar, stabbing them with long sharp knives—even in deep winter this was good country for game. (While hunting they silenced the bells they wore with strips of cloth.) We saw the tracks and spoor of polyhounds, too, but the trails were old ones.

One night, having watched the women see to Hans' leg, I said to Jok:

"He is well enough to travel. It is time we bade you farewell."

He was silent and I did not think he had heard me: the tintinnabulation of the bells was very noisy. I started to repeat myself but he said:

"I was not born of the Tribe."

It did not seem to have anything to do with my own remark but I listened politely. He went on:

"Sometimes strangers are accepted among us. I was such a stranger once."

I still did not take his drift and remained silent. He looked at me, smiling:

"Stay with us, Luke."

I was astonished. I said: "It is a kindness and an honor. But should not the rest of your people be consulted?"

He laughed. "Do you know us so little yet? Each speaks for all."

I said awkwardly: "Then I am grateful for the offer. But I cannot stay."

"Why not? You are happy here."

He spoke with calmness and certainty. And there was more to it than the words by themselves might convey. He meant also that among his people a man would know happiness of a kind that he would find in no other place; and wild though the boast might seem, I could not disbelieve it.

I said: "And Hans?"

"He, as well."

"A dwarf?"

"We would not keep a babe so stunted, but he has grown to manhood. His legs are short but his body is strong. We welcome Hans also."

I shook my head. "It is no good. I must go on."

"For what reason?"

At last he was curious—curious that any should refuse the gift of their comradeship. I hesitated. The hopes and plans of the High Seers would make no sense to him—they meant little enough to me at this moment. So I said nothing of that, but spoke of the wrongs I had suffered: of friendship and trust betrayed, that city lost which was mine by right. Jok listened. At last he said:

"We can heal you of this sickness, Luke."

"Sickness? I am not sick."

"Very sick. Those who have been born in the Tribe would not understand you, but I do. I remember things like jealousy and pride and hatred of one's fellow man. Or woman. They are distant memories, almost forgotten but not quite. The Tribe healed me, and can heal you. Already these wrongs you fancy were done you are less important: is that not true?"

I could not deny it. During recent days I had scarcely thought of Edmund and Blodwen and Harding. My nights had been unbroken, my dreams happy.

"Stay with us," Jok said. "Forget your ambitions and angers. We have much to give you: an end to loneliness and misery, a peace of heart such as you can only guess at now."

That too was true. Even after this short time of living with them I knew it to be so. It was absurd on the face of it that I, who had been Prince of three cities, should be tempted by the thought of living, with neither rank nor glory, among a primitive tribe of hut-dwellers; but I was tempted. To forget all wretchedness of the past, for the first time in my life to be at peace . . .

But I summoned up two faces, hers and his, and summoned my resolution with it. I said harshly:

"You mean well, and I thank you for it. But it does not serve my purpose."

"No?" He put his hand on mine, the touch in itself a token of all he had promised. "Then stay only for a few days longer. Your revenge will wait."

It would wait, but waiting it might die, withered by this warmth of giving and sharing. And I knew that in my deepest heart nothing—no peace or happiness or goodness—counted with me as this did.

I said: "We leave tomorrow."

"So be it." He shook his head slightly. "We could have healed you. Go in what peace you can know. Maybe in the end you will heal yourself; but you will suffer for it."

Since Klan Gothlen was a city without walls, there was no guard to challenge us as we entered it. We walked through the streets, with the domed and spired and turreted buildings rising on either side, their colors looking more gaudy still against the snowy hills beyond. People looked at us with interest as we passed, but that meant nothing. The Wilsh were always inquisitive about new things, new faces. Dirty and travel-worn as we were, it was scarcely likely that we would be recognized as Luke, the slayer of the Bayemot, and his servant Hans.

The guard on the palace did not know me either, until I spoke. Then he dropped his spear and let me through. I asked a footman where I would find the King, and he told me in the red chamber. He would have announced me but I told him I would find my own way there. He bowed and stood aside: my reputation was still a passport in this place. I wondered how much longer that would be true.

It was warm after the cold outside: too warm. I remembered Cymru telling me that in winter they heated the floors with fires that warmed air beneath them. Within moments I was sweating. At the door of the red chamber I was challenged again, and passed again. I went through into a hum of talk, which stopped on my appearance.

Cymru was there, lying among cushions on a couch of crimson velvet matching the crimson of the wall hangings. I saw many others I knew: Kluellan, the Colonel of the Guard, Snake, Cymru's polymuf Chancellor with tentacles for fingers and strangely jointed limbs, Bevili, the Perfumer Royal with his scarlet lips . . . a dozen or more nobles of the city. Snake was the first to address me. He said:

"Luke of Winchester! So our hero returns. But you look as though you have had a hard journey here."

I had, I knew, offended against Wilsh etiquette by coming into the King's presence dirty and disheveled. But it seemed to me this was no occasion for etiquette. I eased the pack from my shoulders and let it drop.

Cymru said: "What brings you to us in the full of winter? And in such a state?" He raised himself from his cushions and stared at me. His dark face had no smile of welcome. "Where is Blodwen?"

"In Winchester, sire."

He frowned. "You have left her there, unguarded?"

"I had no choice."

His eyes went small. "Do you say so? We put her into your protection."

"Will you hear me, sire?"

Cymru said grimly: "We will hear you."

I told my story, sparing nothing. Cymru and the Wilsh nobles watched me as I spoke. There was shock and amazement in their faces but I could not read what else. When I finished there was a pause before Cymru spoke.

"You have lost your city," he said, "and you have lost Blodwen to one of those Captains who deposed you. What brings you here? Do you seek an audience for your tears? Or perhaps a pension?"

"Neither, sire. I seek an army."

His cold eyes studied me and he pulled his grizzled beard.

"You beg our aid?"

I shook my head. "I beg nothing, sire. I demand it."

"Demand?" He was incredulous. "Of me?"

"She was your gift," I said, "in return for slaying the Bayemot I gave you thanks. I took her in good faith. She played me false and, through her, enemies have stolen my city from me. In breaking faith with me she dishonors you, and all your people. She is your daughter, Cymru. I demand your aid so that I may kill her and her lover."

His face had changed while I was saying this. Coldness and surprise gave way to heat and anger. By the time I finished it was full of rage. He would have me killed, I thought, and vowed I would not die quietly. I would take some of them with me, perhaps Cymru himself, before they cut me down.

But the rage and anger were not for me. He said:

"All you say is truth. You will have your army. And I will ride with you when you go to take your revenge."

EIGHT

THE BATTLE OF AMESBURY

FROM THAT MOMENT BLODWEN'S NAME WAS never mentioned in Cymru's court.

They were good haters, the Wilsh. I remember what Blodwen herself had said, as she rode between Edmund and me on the day of the hunt, the day of the killing of the Bayemot. "In our country when a man makes an enemy it is forever." She was Cymru's only child. He had loved her and indulged her greatly. But she had dishonored him, and that was enough. I think he would have watched her die with a smile on his lips.

Snake told me, and I believed him, that my own

life had hung by a thread in the red room that afternoon. Had I shown weakness, he said, Cymru would have ordered my death because of the news I brought. I would have been a reminder of his disgrace, to be removed without pity.

But his acceptance of my vow to take revenge, and his joining with me in it, set me even higher in his regard than during my first visit to Klan Gothlen. Snake told me this also, before I had truly realized it.

"She was his daughter," he said, "but he would wash his hands in her blood. He would have killed you had you begged or flinched; and now you are his son. I do not say it lightly. Fond as he was of her, that is a lack he has always felt, and you fill it. No man who is wise will cross Luke of Winchester in this city from now on." He smiled. "It would be almost as bad as defying the King himself."

He spoke without rancor. He was a devious man, as I suppose a Chancellor should be, but I had come to respect him. His manner showed no resentment but no false flattery either. Behind the slyness of the surface he showed the world, there was some honesty.

And the truth of his forecast of my preeminence in the King's favor was borne out the next day. I was talking of the new tactics that would be required with the use of Sten guns, and Kluellan interrupted. He took something I said as showing ignorance of the qualities of Wilsh troops, and indignantly challenged what he thought was a slur. As Colonel of the Guard he commanded the army in the field, directly under the King, and thought himself its spokesman. I held my peace, but Cymru said:

"Enough, Kluellan! You are older than Luke, but can learn from him." Others were present: Captains and civilian nobles. He raised his voice. "Luke is my lieutenant in this enterprise. I would have that kept in mind by all of you."

As I had guessed would be the case, the Wilsh were not shocked by the weapon I had brought them, but fascinated. At the demonstration I gave they clapped and shouted with delight. I had had a wooden target set up, but this did not satisfy Cymru. Snake, with his usual care for his monarch's future pleasures, had arranged for wild boar to be caught and kept in pens within the city; so that whenever the weather should prove fair enough to tempt

Cymru to a hunt there would be quarry to be released. Cymru called for one of these to be loosed now, at the end of the narrow yard in which we stood.

It was a half-grown boar, not polybeast as far as I could see. It stood in front of the trap from which it had been set free, undecided what to do, alarmed probably by the noisy chatter of the Wilsh nobles.

"Now, Luke," Cymru cried, "show us what this gun of yours does to that young tusker."

Except for food, one killed beasts only in sport; and there was no sport in firing bullets into a defenseless and most likely frightened animal. It was not even moving. But I remembered that Cymru's idea of a hunt was firing crossbow bolts from behind wooden covers. And it was Cymru I relied on to help get me back my city and my pride. I wasted no time in hesitation but raised the Sten gun to my waist and fired a burst. The boar gave one sharp squeal as the bullets smashed it to the ground, then lay there silent in its gore.

The Wilsh nobles broke into loud applause. Many, even ladies, rushed forward to examine the dead animal, and I saw one lady dabble her delicate fingers in its blood. I hid my disgust. These were my people until I won my own city back.

Cymru said: "Have it taken to Lewin." That was the Master Cook. "We will dine on roast boar tonight. Tell him I shall require one of his best sauces to go with it."

Hans turned armorer; and I wondered what old Rudi would have thought of it, recalling his regret when Hans, his last son, chose not to follow him to the forge. It was, of course, a very different kind of armory. In the King's name I had put Hans in complete charge of the making of the Sten guns. He was in any case the only man who had the knowledge for it. I could use the weapon, but I could as easily have flown up to the top of one of the Wilsh mountains as make it.

He found good and willing craftsmen here: not only dwarfs but polymufs and true men also. When I visited them in the forge-house I found a great bustle of activity, with the roar of flame and the clang and hammer of steel added to by a clamor of voices. Unlike our Winchester dwarfs, who were silent workers for the most part, the Wilsh could not even shape steel without chattering; and there were times when, one of them first taking up a tune, they would all burst out into singing.

I asked him one day how matters were progressing. He said:

"Very well, sire. They are quick to learn."

"By spring . . ."

"We shall have two hundred and fifty guns for you. More maybe. And ammunition enough and to spare. Will that do?"

"It will do. Hans, without you I could do nothing. These Wilsh soldiers are better than I once thought, but with equal weapons they would have small chance against our warriors of Winchester, and there are other territories to get through first. I think all the cities will fight against an army that comes from beyond the Burning Lands, whether it offers defiance or no."

Hans looked at me. "I think so, too, sire."

"I made you a warrior," I said, "and now you have become my armorer to help me. It will not be for long. When spring comes and the guns are ready you can be a warrior again. And this time one of my Captains."

I had thought he would be overjoyed. For a dwarf to be a warrior was a marvelous thing; but this would make him noble.

He said slowly: "It is a great honor, sire. But . . ."

I was amazed. "But what?"

"I am not sure I desire it."

His doubts did not stem from lack of courage, as I well knew. He had as brave a heart as any man I had met.

I said: "Why, Hans? Because you would be commanding Wilsh, against our own people?"

"No. I serve you against anyone. And I am making guns to kill them."

"Then why?"

He picked a Sten gun up and gazed at it. "I cannot remember a time when I did not want to be a warrior. There was a place where I could climb the citadel wall and stay there hidden, watching the drilling and jousting and sword play. The longing was greater because it was an impossible thing."

He put the gun down and looked at me.

"By your hand, sire, the impossible became a reality. I fought with you at Petersfield and Romsey. But that was in the old way, on horseback, with sword and shield. It will not be the same to carry a gun at one's hip and kill a man a hundred yards away—a man maybe who has not even seen you. I will make the guns but I do not think I want to use them."

"You will not refuse to go with me when we ride south, Hans?"

"No, sire." He smiled. "I will not do that. Not then or ever. I go wherever you go."

I worked hard that winter, drilling and organizing the army, making plans and preparations for the campaign to come. I rose early and rested little through a long day. This was no hardship. In work I could forget my shames, and keep at bay those specters that otherwise filled vacancy to mock and jeer at me. There were hours on end when I did not think of Blodwen, nights when I went to bed so tired that I did not dream.

Cymru remonstrated with me for this unceasing labor, though I think he was impressed by it. He asked me to take things more easily, then begged, at last commanded. This was at the Christmas Feast, which the Wilsh kept far more lavishly even than we had done in Winchester. For twelve days there was a round of feasts and balls, masques and concerts and visitings, a vast gluttony of eating and drinking. Lewin and his minions produced mountains of food, most elaborately prepared, glazed and sauced. On one great table he set up a pyramid, ten feet high, of meats cooked and carved in strange patterns of shape and hue, the whole thing topped by the head of the biggest boar I had ever seen. A polybeast, of course, but that counted for nothing in this land.

On the chief day of the Feast there was a procession of Christians through the streets of the city, ending up at their church, a huge building bearing no fewer than seven large onion domes, which they called the Cathedral. Cymru and his court joined in the procession as it passed the palace and walked the last hundred yards with it, before actually going into the church immediately behind the Bishop.

When Cymru told me of this, taking it for granted that I would go with them, I said in surprise:

"But you are not a Christian."

"I am not one of the White Witches, either, but I attend their grand coven at midsummer. And preside at the feast the farmers give at harvest, though I am not a farmer. Amongst us the King is father to his people as long as they obey the law. And the Christians do that as well as any."

"In our lands they give trouble by protesting against war and executions." I remembered a bitter freezing morning in Salisbury and myself punished as an Acolyte who had disgraced the Seers' cloth. "Even against men being put into the stocks."

"They make no protests here," Cymru said. "And their Christmas worshiping is worth attending for the music."

So I walked beside him from the palace to the Cathedral. Snow fell lightly and it was cold in the open when one had become used to the heated floors of the palace, but we were well wrapped in furs. So too, I saw, were the Christians. They looked fat and prosperous, quite different from the ragged starvelings I had known in the south. There were fewer than a hundred of them. I said to Cymru:

"Is this their full number?"

"All who can will attend the Christmas worship," he said. "Their numbers dwindle. Forty years ago, when I walked here beside my father, there were three times as many. But their music is still excellent."

Listening, I supposed it was. I found it florid stuff, with much contrast between boys' trebles and deep booming basses: there were almost as many in the choir as in the audience. But I knew nothing of music, anyway. I let my mind wander to watch the others in the church. Sitting on their high-backed benches they looked even fatter and richer than before. I wondered what our Winchester Bishop would make of them. They looked far worthier citizens than his own rabble. And yet, Cymru had said, their numbers dwindled. It was not easy to account for it.

I put the question to their Bishop later, when he came to the feast at the palace. His name was Griffis and I had seen him at court before. For such visits he put off his Christian robes and his elegance outdid the majority of Cymru's nobles, a notable achievement. He spoke elegantly too; more slowly than was usual among the Wilsh and with what was thought to be great wit. I could not always see the jest myself, but the Wilsh nobles round him were quick to laugh.

He said: "Numbers do not of themselves give distinction." From a tray proffered by a page he took a small roast bird and crunched it delicately. "It is sometimes an honor to be part of a minority." He glanced sideways at me, smiling. "Did you not find yourself in this case with the Captains of your city?"

Someone tittered. I had heard this Bishop on other occasions dripping malice from his slightly twisted mouth. The Wilsh nobles were nearly all gossips, but he outdid them in that also. I said coldly:

"You have a merry wit, Bishop." He inclined his head, smiling still. "I must tell the King that you find treachery a good subject for jesting. Maybe he will laugh with you."

He looked at me quickly to see if I were jesting in my turn. When I stared heavily back at him he quickly changed his tune. I had misunderstood him, he said, but it was for him to apologize for the misunderstanding. From that he went on fulsomely in flattery of me. It was laid on like the grease which still rimmed his lips from the bird he had been eating, smooth and oily. After a moment or two I nodded, and turned my back. It was discourtesy, but I could stand no more of the man.

I thought of the Bishop of Winchester, talking boldly about forbidden things, speaking up to an Acolyte in the presence of his Prince. And thinking of it I thought of who else had been there that night, saw her again scolding me and then sweetly pleading as she told me whom she had asked to dine with us. And sickness filled my heart as the Wilsh nobles chattered and laughed and gorged themselves all round me. I left the room and went up to the quiet of my chamber. The double windows were shut. I opened them and stepped out onto the balcony. The river was frozen except where it tumbled down its horseshoe falls, barely visible in the darkness. Beyond it lights flickered from the hundred towers of Klan Gothlen, and whispers of music came in on the night air.

The cold was sharp against my skin and memory a knife in my mind. I clenched the freezing balustrade with my fingers. Soon, thanks be to the Great, the feasting days would be over and it would be time to work again.

At last winter ended, and the army could ride south. We set off with banners and pennants flying in a stiff breeze that blew down from the mountains and still had ice in it. The citizens cheered us from their towers and balconies and thronged the streets to watch us pass. Apart from the scouts, Cymru rode in the van and I beside him.

It was a leisurely progress. We could not travel at any great pace because of the baggage train, which was enormous. I had been for reducing it to the minimum, but on this one point Cymru overrode me. So we went laden with gear of all kinds—tents for the nobles, a pavilion for Cymru himself—and a great store of food and drink. This at least we consumed as we made our way south. But we still took far more than an army in the field needed—and far more, as I pointed out to Cymru, than we should be able to take with us over the pass through the Burning Lands.

We were sitting in his pavilion which had been set up close by the river. Our camp stretched for half a mile along the valley. Had there been any possible enemy I would have wanted it more tightly disposed, but on this side of the Burning Lands there was none to challenge the might of Cymru's army.

Cymru laughed. "We shall travel lightly when we

need to, Luke, but until the need arises we Wilsh will have our comforts. Could Lewin have prepared a dinner such as we had tonight without his mountain of pots and pans and his own army of scullions?"

I said: "The contrast may come hard."

He smiled at me strangely. "You do not understand us yet. We are a people of contrasts." He looked across the river. "A people who smile and talk lightly, but our hearts are extreme."

In love and hatred I thought, but did not say. We did not talk of her but her presence was between us.

"You do not understand us, Luke," Cymru said, "but perhaps you are more like us than you think."

Bats swooped low in the dusk over the hurrying waters. We sat in silence as the night came on.

We passed the place where the polyhounds had surrounded Hans and me, and the valley of the Tribe. I wondered if Jok and the others were watching our progress from cover; I saw no sign of them. We passed the village of the building rats, deserted still and almost overgrown with weeds and saplings, and that other village from which I had been taken, as a sacrificial victim, to the Eyrie of the Sky People.

We skirted the forest in which Edmund and I, in an upper room of a crumbling palace, had found a skeleton dressed in the moldering clothes of the past, and a gold box, and a painting of an old man, done with a skill no painter of our time could equal. And so we came at last to the black desolation where trees and plants withered in the heat, where there were only rocks and steaming pools, and the air was choked with dust from the clouds of smoke that hung over the jagged peaks of the Burning Lands.

We left the baggage train there, along with Lewin and his scullions. The horses' legs were wrapped about with asbestos cloth, and we took nothing with us but our weapons. Cymru himself put aside his velvet cloaks and wore a leather jerkin, armored with slats of steel. I was surprised by the difference it made in him: he looked a warrior now.

I went across the pass first, leading the scouts. I had decided to bring the army over in units of twenty, to avoid confusion. It made it a long business. We had started in early morning but at nightfall a quarter of the army was still on the other side.

If we had been attacked during this maneuver we

would have been massacred; but I had no fear of it. There was no dwelling within five miles of the pass; no blade of grass on which a wandering shepherd might feed his flock. There was only a barren desert with the Burning Lands between. The next day the rest of the army came over. We lost one horse that fell and threw its rider and had to be destroyed, having broken a leg. But another warrior picked up the horseman and got him across with nothing worse than a few burns.

When we had gathered our forces, we rode south. Kluellan had been in favor of taking the nearest town to use as a base, but I had vetoed it. That town was Marlborough. It was part of Oxford's kingdom and for more reasons than one I did not want to get embroiled with Oxford. So we bypassed it and made for Salisbury.

We had brought little in the way of provisions, ammunition for the guns being the more important consideration, and so we had to live off the land. The villages through which we passed were forced to give us food. In return we did them no harm. At one place there was a scuffle between one of the Wilsh soldiers and a girl. I do not know what caused it—the soldier swore his innocence—but Kluellan had him flogged on the spot.

From the moment of first contact, of course, pigeons had taken word of our presence, and it had spread far and wide by now. I knew they would have heard of it in Winchester, and wondered what Blodwen would think of my return at the head of her father's army. She and her lover might have had many laughs together during the winter, over poor banished Luke. This news would not give them much to laugh at.

We followed the Avon valley and so passed within a few miles of Sanctuary. I did not try to contact the High Seers. They had given me a weapon but I had won an army myself. I no longer needed either them or their Science.

It was while we were camped between Sanctuary and the town of Amesbury that the scouts brought word of an enemy. The army of Salisbury had ridden north to challenge us. So we prepared for battle, and the next morning fought it.

Our army numbered more than a thousand, of which three hundred were armed with Sten guns.

These left their horses tethered and advanced on foot. I watched it from high ground, west of the river. They looked like peasants as they walked across the green fields, specked white and gold with buttercups and daisies. In front of them, holding a slight rise, the men of Salisbury sat their horses, whose occasional snorts and whinnies came thinly through the air. Their banners of red and black blew bravely in a breeze from the north. It was a fine sight. I felt my blood thrill to it. The men on foot seemed puny in comparison.

The horsemen were preparing themselves for the charge. I saw the bugler lift his instrument to his lips and heard the harsh notes blare out, my horse twitching under me at the distant sound. For a moment, despite all I knew of the weapon I had armed them with, I did not believe the Wilsh footmen could withstand their onslaught.

They moved, slowly at first but gathering speed and momentum. I watched my own troops and anxiously waited. The Captains had been told to let them come to fifty yards and then, on the command of one Captain, fire together. They had practiced this against their own horsemen, firing the bullets into the ground in front of them; but practice, as any warrior knew, was not the same as battle. If they fired prematurely and raggedly, it was possible that all might be lost.

But the months of drilling and discipline brought their reward now. They stood like rocks while the line of horsemen thundered down. I guessed the distance separating them as best I could. Two hundred yards, a hundred, seventy-five . . . Then the single cry: "Fire!"—and after that not one tongueless stammering giant but hundreds of them. The valley rocked with the noise.

And as though they had crashed into a steel rope, drawn across their front, the line of horsemen stumbled and fell. Maybe a score rode on a few more yards, ten, even twenty, and were picked off one by one. None reached the soldiers with the guns.

I raised my arm. From behind, the Wilsh horsemen charged in their turn, the footmen giving way to let them through. Their swords flashed as they rode down on those men of Salisbury who had risen from their dead or dying horses. Some did their best to fight, but their case was helpless. They were cut down with scarcely more trouble than a girl might take to pluck a flower. Soon they dropped their swords in surrender. From the bugle call to this instant, no more than ten minutes had passed.

Within an hour I had a visitor. He came from the north with a single troop of horse, no more than thirty men. His standard bearer carried the white flag of truce. It was Eric of Oxford.

He dismounted and gave me greeting, and I returned it.

He said: "I had news of your coming, Luke. And news earlier of what happened in Winchester. Why did you not come to me? I would have helped you."

"Your father might not have made me welcome."

"He would have known nothing." I looked at him in inquiry. "He was gravely ill even then and confined to bed. He died in November."

"And you are Prince of Oxford? I have failed in duty."

I gave him the formal bow which a Captain should make to a ruler. He laughed.

"Enough of that! If what I hear is true you command a greater army than mine. But you may still welcome help to win back your city. I told you once: when I can help, I will. I can do so now."

"It is an army of barbarians," I said, "from beyond the Burning Lands. Have you heard that also?"

"All the more need for the support of friends! Then no one can say you required barbarians to regain your own. It looks better if you have an ally close to home. I can bring my army here within a week. Can you hold off from battle till then?"

"You are too late, Eric. The battle has been fought."

"Fought, you say?"

He looked at the bustle of the Wilsh camp around us. I said:

"And won. Would you see the field?"

He rode in silence with me. I heard him draw breath as we came in sight of the ugly rampart that marked the scene of carnage. It was made up of the broken bodies of horses in their hundreds, mingled with the bodies of men. In among them moved those Wilsh I had detailed to end the sufferings of any horses that still lived. I think probably they had already finished that work for no horse moved or cried. They were engaged on a more congenial occupation: stripping the dead warriors of Salisbury of their rings and ornaments.

Some ten yards from the wall of horror, Eric reined in.

"I have never seen slaughter approaching this," he said. "What casualties did your Wilsh have?"

"None. None serious, at least. A few have minor wounds."

He shook his head. "It is beyond believing. It is said the Spirits protect you. But do they rain death from the skies on armies that take the field against you?"

I told him of the Sten guns. I did not say where they came from, leaving him to think it was a device of the Wilsh. He said:

"They are machines, then."

I asked: "Is that so hard a thing to hear, for one who told me he looked for change from old and stupid ways?"

"I looked for change; not for a rotting mountain of dead horses. Your enemies are men. Did you need to have your soldiers kill these poor beasts so mercilessly?"

"The horses are a bigger target, their riders help-less once they are brought down. The soldiers fired at them by my command. These are the right tactics for winning a battle with such a weapon."

"I believe you. But is there honor in such a victory?"

"What is honor?" I said. "They stripped mine from me in Harding's house, sitting round an oak table. But I live, to take my revenge."

Eric was silent, staring at the carnage. Directly opposite us a stallion, a magnificent bay, thrust its head upward to the sky, jaws open in a silent scream.

I said: "The old battles achieved nothing: you told me that in Winchester. They had horses and honor but they brought no resolution. Things will be differ-ent from now on. There will be no room for horses or honor in the battles we shall fight, but we shall have victories of a kind men have not known before."

Eric turned his horse's head away. He said:

"All this may well be true. I bid you farewell, then, Luke."

"You will not bring your army south to join us?"

He smiled. "I was mistaken. You have no need of help."

"And the alliance you offered me?"

"Farewell, Luke."

I rode with him a little way. "Will you fight against me?"

"Am I a fool?" he said. "I have seen your victory."

NINE

THE WALLS OF WINCHESTER

SALISBURY OPENED ITS GATES TO US IN shock. I put a garrison there and moved on. I left forty men and that was more than was needed; because I left twenty Sten guns with them. I had no fear of an uprising after the army had gone.

We took the road to the east. I had not intended to attack Romsey but their army came on us as we crossed the valley of the Test. They aimed to take us by surprise, riding out of the shelter of woods as we approached the river and clearly hoping to drive us into it.

They appeared to have some success at the outset. Their charge broke through our flank, and I heard their cry of triumph: "Romsey! Romsey!" But the flank had given way on my instructions. Our Sten gun troops were in the center. They had no time to dismount, but they wreaked a fair havoc from horseback. The attack crumpled and broke. Those that were not brought down scattered and fled to the woods from which they had started.

Our own horsemen pursued them, killing many, but I called them back by bugle. The victory was decisive enough; and a rabble fleeing back to the city served us better than unnecessary slaughter. It would be easy enough to take Romsey, and other things came first. The road to Winchester lay open.

The banners of the army that rode out of the woods had all been yellow and black, and there were no men of Winchester among the fallen. This meant that Romsey had freed itself, or been set free by Harding and the rest. But although they must have heard by now how we had destroyed the army of Salisbury, they had still ridden against us alone rather than wait and join with Winchester.

Cymru spoke of it. "These are a strange people. Out of resentment, you think? But we are foreign and invade their lands. Does it not make sense to combine together when there is a threat to all?"

I tried to explain the way of it to him, but with small success. He could not conceive what it might be like to live as a citizen of one free and independent city amongst many, to nourish rivalries through generations. He came after all from a single city, an oasis of culture and prosperity surrounded by lands that were savage but offered no threat. There were no divisions among the Wilsh, or none that mattered.

Cymru shrugged. "Well, it serves our purpose. Though if all their cities sent their armies against us together, I do not think it would make much difference. This is a mighty weapon you have given us, Luke."

I looked at the mound of death beside the river.

"Mighty indeed. Nothing can stand against it."

"I have one regret."

"What is that?"

"That we lose you when you regain your city."

He had said fulsome things about me in the past,

as the Wilsh commonly did; but now he spoke from the heart.

I said: "There will be commerce between us. I shall visit you in Klan Gothlen."

Cymru shook his head. "It is a long journey. And you will be well occupied here. But no man may command another's destiny. It is enough that we share this mission. We shall take your city for you and avenge the insult that concerns us both."

It was raining as we came down into the Itchen valley, a feathery drifting rain that slowly soaked to the skin. We rode past the water meadows where on a summer's day—so long ago but less than a year gone by—Edmund had played the lute and sung to Blodwen while I rode from them, foolishly content. Now the fine rain washed over the grass under a weeping sky of gray.

Our scouts reported the army of Winchester ahead of us. They had drawn up west of the river in ordinary battle array. I said to the scout who told me:

"Are you sure of this? Their full army?"

"We have covered the ground well, Lord. I think

if there was a single man in hiding we would have found him."

I did not doubt it: the Wilsh made cunning scouts. Still it was hard to believe. They would have heard what happened to the warriors of Salisbury and Romsey. Surely they were not such fools as to stand in the open and wait for us to attack?

And yet when we came within view of them my heart was moved by the sight. The troops were set out in classic fashion, each with its banner of blue and gold: Captains, standard-bearers, lancers with their spears at rest, and behind them the swordsmen. It was a brave challenge to those who came against them—a challenge to battle in the old way, right arm against right arm, steel against steel: honor an equal prize with victory.

For a moment I was tempted to accept it, and to lead my Wilsh horsemen into the charge. But too many things had happened, and too much was at stake. I kept the horsemen back. The Sten gunners were already quietly moving into position on high ground to the east. One of the high-roads of our ancestors ran there. It had been a railway once and steam engines had pulled carriages along it, taking people to far places at many times the speed of a galloping horse. Now it was overgrown with bushes and trees, and gave good cover.

They could still have attacked us while the Sten gunners were taking up their places. It would have made no difference in the end, but as with the men of Romsey they might have gained an advantage at the start. But they did not move. They were waiting until our own disposition was complete. According to custom we should sound a bugle to show our readiness. Then they would attack.

Why did they do this? I wondered. Out of folly? It might be so, but they were men I knew, and knew to be hard-headed. Nor could I think they would really believe that I would accept the challenge to fight on equal terms. If I had not spared Salisbury and Romsey, who had done me no real harm, why should I spare them?

I think it was more from resignation and despair. They could see nothing facing them except defeat; but at least they would go down in ancient fashion, fighting as the armies of Winchester had fought for generations. Perhaps it was folly, but it had grandeur in it.

My Sten gunners were ready. I made a sign to the bugler. He sounded the call and it was answered. A quarter of a mile away the line of horsemen began to move toward us.

This time I had told the Sten gunners to hold their fire until a command from me, as shown by a second blast on the bugle. The bugler rode at my side, ready for my word. In front of us the line came on, through the drizzling rain; from a walk to a canter and so to full gallop.

When they were a hundred yards from us they would be not much more than fifty yards from the gunners, thereafter moving away from them as they closed with us. It was that moment I was waiting for. I watched the distance narrow, the word ready in my mouth. When the line drew level with that stunted tree . . . I knew it well, had climbed it as a boy. The horsemen thundered on. They approached the tree; they reached it. I tried to cry my order. Ice blocked my throat and would let no word pass.

They rode in savage fury and their battle cries

shattered the sky. I tried to speak again, and failed again. If they smashed into us with this impetus the Wilsh, I knew, would not withstand them: no horsemen could. Even at that moment I felt a pride in them.

They were not much more than fifty yards away. I could see the faces of men I knew: Blaine, Nicoll, Stuart. And in the center, mouth open in a yell, Edmund, who had been my friend. It was then that the ice cracked. I spoke, and the bugler blew, and at the first savage note my tongueless giants stammered out their hate.

Dozens fell but the rest came on. The guns could only fire for a few moments or they would rake us too. The line was full of gaps but it reached us. Then everything was forgotten in the clash of sword on sword.

I remember little of the battle itself. I do not know who I struck down, nor how many, nor who it was that gave me the thrust in the shoulder that all but unhorsed me. I do not know how long it lasted. Time has no meaning in a battle and this was a battle of the old kind, the last such there would ever be. All was slash and counterslash, cries of men in pain or triumph, the snort and squeal of horses, nerve-wrenching scrape and clang of steel, the wetness of rain and sweat and blood . . .

They drew back at last. Late though the command had been, the guns had taken dire toll of them before they reached us. Only desperate courage had enabled them to come to grips with our horsemen after that. They broke and scattered and fled under the shoulder of Catherine's Hill to the distant East Gate.

I did not take my men and ride after them, but let them go.

The surgeon came to see to my wound. I told him it would wait, dismissing him with anger when he persisted. I walked between the bodies of the fallen. Some of the Wilsh were unfamiliar to me but there was not a face among the dead of Winchester I did not know. Barnes I saw, and the trooper who had taken my arm when he arrested me in my brother's name. Foster, whom Hans had come near killing in the barracks on the night of the victory feast, lay sprawled on his back—now truly dead. I saw Edmund's brother, Charles, with his head in a bloody puddle, eyes staring in surprise.

And I saw Harding. There was no mark on him, either of bullet or sword, but his horse lay dead of bullet wounds beside him. Harding's head drooped at an unlikely angle. He had been thrown when his horse fell, I guessed, and broken his neck. I looked long at him. He had always been a slight man and now seemed very small, a child grown old. I felt no pity, but no joy either.

There was another body near. A bullet had caught him high up on the forehead, making a single blackened hole through which his life had ebbed. It was Wilson, my father's oldest companion, who had refused a Captaincy from him but taken it from me; not because he wanted the honor but to protect me better. Wilson, the one Captain who had voted against the rest when they condemned me to exile.

I looked and turned away. I would have howled like a dog but the ice was back in my throat. I stumbled through the rain to where Cymru and the surgeon waited.

Greene and Ripon were two of the three who came to parley: the third was Edmund.

I received them sitting beside Cymru, with Snake

in attendance also. I offered them cakes and ale.

"It is a good brew," I said. "It was made on my father's farm, not half a mile from here. But I can give you ale from your own farms if you would prefer it."

"We want no ale," Greene said. "We seek to know your terms."

"That is easily done. I want nothing but my own: my city and the bride who was given to me by this her father."

"A city is not something that can be given," Greene said, "except by the will of its citizens. This is well known in civilized lands. Your father first seduced us from that course by taking Petersfield, and under your rule we strayed still further into error. We are paying for it now and know we must pay heavily. But we will not yield our freedom."

Cymru said: "And my daughter? Will you yield her, to her father?"

It was Edmund who answered. "A free lady may not be given up, any more than a city may. If she wishes to come to you, she will. No one will force her."

Cymru stared at him with black anger. "Your

comrade talks of seducing, but what of you? You, who ate my bread, seduced my daughter from your Prince and friend. And do you chatter now of freedom?"

Greene said: "This gets us nowhere. We acknowledge defeat. We will say nothing of the way the victory was won. We will pay you gold—all the gold we have in the city. Our wives will strip the rings from their fingers to give you. Take your ransom, and let us live in peace."

I shook my head. "We want no gold. No more than the gates of the city. One gate will do. And the Lady Blodwen restored to her father."

"To her father," Edmund said, "or to a man she hates?"

It told me only what I knew already but the shaft went home. The wound in my shoulder was nothing to it.

Greene said: "You will get neither. And our walls are high. Prince Stephen, Edmund's father, saw to that."

"In the end you will yield," I said. "It does not matter to us whether it is soon or late. The suffering is on your side."

"You will starve us, then?" Greene said. "We have wheat and cattle. When they have gone we will kill our horses and eat them. And after that we will hunt out rats for our suppers. And after that if we must starve then starve we will. But while there is any strength in our arms you will not come into the city."

"Brave words," I said. "But the promise is easier made than kept."

They were ready to go. Cymru said to Edmund:

"A message for my daughter."

"What is it, sire?"

"Send her her father's curse."

Edmund bowed. "She is too gentle to return it to you. But I do it for her."

They sent the Wilsh soldiers who had been Blodwen's bodyguard out to us. We kept the siege all summer. Kluellan, guided by Snake, proved an excellent quartermaster. We fed off the city farms first; then sent our troops to forage far afield. It was still no easy life, especially compared with the luxury of Klan Gothlen, and I was surprised by how well Cymru and the Wilsh nobles endured it. I had thought there might be mutterings, talk of abandoning it all, but there was none.

Much hung on Cymru himself of course, and his purpose did not waver. When I spoke of it once, he said:

"We have come a long way, Luke. Too far to abandon a purpose so nearly won."

If the paralysis had not gripped my throat when the command to fire was needed, or if I had pursued them as they fled toward the East Gate, our victory would have been sealed already. We both knew that but he had never charged me with it. I said:

"They are a stubborn people, sire."

Cymru laughed. "We Wilsh can be stubborn, too! And this hard life does us good. We have had too soft a time of it in the past."

But all the same I brooded unhappily on the future. We could not keep the army in the field in winter. It was true we had a base in Salisbury on which we could fall back; but that would be a retreat and the thought sickened me. Nor was I confident, however high their morale stayed at present, that the Wilsh would cheerfully endure a winter in a foreign city, with the prospect of resuming the siege of another foreign city in the spring. A soldier must leave home and family when his monarch requires it;

but it does not mean that he forgets them. And his longing for them does not weaken with absence but grows stronger.

Then one day in late summer a man in black robes, on a white horse, rode into the camp. It was Murphy, the High Seer.

He greeted me, and said: "You look well, Luke. Older and tougher, but well. And this is the army which you abandoned us to find. We have heard great things of it. I once doubted that you would take a Wilsh army against your own city and with such weapons as we gave you. I am glad to find I was wrong."

I shrugged. "We have come so far, but here we stay. You can kill men in the field with Sten guns, but they do little harm to the stone walls of a city."

"You should have asked us for another weapon, then."

I looked at him sharply. "Is there such? Big guns, you mean? But can they be made with the materials we have?"

"No," Murphy said, "or at least not easily. But there is a thing called a mortar. It was devised for use against forts, as a siege weapon. It throws bombs at a high angle to explode against the walls."

I said doubtfully: "The walls of Winchester are not only high but strongly made."

"Have you seen a thrush with a snail?" Murphy asked. "It will pick the shell up and throw it against the stone. The shell does not break at that first impact. But the bird picks it up and throws it again. It will throw it a score of times, fifty if necessary. In the end the shell is weakened. It breaks and the thrush gets its reward. We have many more than fifty bombs for you. I promise you: the walls of the city will crack like the snail's shell."

I said: "Where is this mortar, Murphy?"

He smiled. "You will not have long to wait. It will be here tomorrow. I rode ahead to tell you of it."

"Get me this city," I said, "and you will have your Science back. I promise that."

"Within two days it will be yours."

The mortar came at noon the next day, on a cart drawn by two horses. It was not at all like the cannons which the Prince of Petersfield had used against my father's army. They had been long and slender of muzzle. The mortar was a squat affair, wide-mouthed, almost as broad across as it was long. It looked a poor instrument to break down the walls which Stephen had spent five years building up.

And the first bomb it cast fell short, dropping in marshy ground beneath the city's wall, throwing up mud and water but doing no harm except to the frogs that dwelt there. Robb and Gunter had brought it, and they and Murphy consulted together and shifted the angle of the muzzle. The second bomb burst halfway up the wall, and the Wilsh who were watching raised a cheer at the sight. It died as the smoke cleared away, showing the wall undamaged.

The High Seers adjusted the muzzle again. The third bomb struck high up, just under the parapet. Robb said with satisfaction:

"I think we have it."

Murphy had brought field glasses with him. These had lenses like spectacles but the lenses were doubled and much stronger. They made small distant objects seem large and close. I was using them, and I said:

"There is no damage there."

"Not yet," Murphy said. "It is a lucky thrush that gets its snail at the first blow. But we have the range and it is only a question of time."

The mortar boomed again, and went on booming. After about an hour the glasses showed cracks and pittings in the wall. After two hours the parapet above that point collapsed, and the Wilsh cheered again.

The afternoon had turned warm, and the mortar itself gave off heat. Murphy wiped sweat from his brow.

"You were right. The walls are strong. But we have made a breach. Now it is only a question of hammering away at it."

"How long, do you think?"

"Not today. But by noon tomorrow there will be a hole you can take your army through."

"I can wait for that," I said.

The angle of the muzzle had to be adjusted as the breach in the wall widened and deepened. The bombardment went on until the light failed with dusk. The top half of the wall had collapsed by then, but the lower half still held.

. . .

In the morning Hans came to my tent as usual to wake me, but I was awake already. He stood in the opening, silhouetted against the faint light of dawn. I said:

"This is a good day, Hans. Today we shall see our homes again."

"Yes, sire," he said. "Sire, there is someone who would see you; from the city."

"Another deputation?" I stood up, yawning. "They are early risers. But they will get no better terms for that."

"One man only. He who was an Acolyte."

"Who was . . . ?"

I left the tent. Martin stood there, waiting. He had grown his hair and he wore ordinary clothes instead of the Acolyte's black robe. Apart from that he seemed little different. He was thin, but he had never had much flesh on his bones.

I clasped his hand and said:

"Martin! I am glad to see you. How did you get here?"

"Through the Christians' tunnel under the walls."

That was the tunnel my brother Peter had used to take the city back from the Romsey army. I had not attempted to use it because it was known now, and they could pick my men off one by one as they came out. But I had not blocked it either.

I said: "You have been in the city? I thought you went to the High Seers in the Sanctuary under the rains of London?"

"I went there, but did not stay."

"Could they not give you what you were seeking, either?"

"No." He smiled. "I went a long journey and found what I sought in the place from which I started. But maybe the journey was necessary for all that."

"What did you find?"

"Truth. The truth that is my truth. I am a Christian, Luke."

I stared and laughed. "You jest! The truth you looked for was the truth of Science. Do you remember the old book you showed me, under the Ruins, with pictures of machines, and how bitterly you spoke against superstition and lies? Do you remember how you pleaded with me to flee the city with Ezzard, so that the mission of the High Seers could be preserved and Science at last brought back? Will you tell me now that you believe in this tale of a god born in a stable, out of the body of a maiden, who walked the earth performing wonders such as the Seers work in the Seance Hall, who died on a cross but three days later walked again, and who at last rose into the sky to sit among the stars and judge all men? Will you tell me this?"

"All that and more. Because Science gave no meaning to my life, but this does. But I did not come here to talk of Christian beliefs, Luke. I come to plead for the city which bore us both."

"Do you? Who sent you—Edmund, who stole my lady from me, and then the city itself?"

I spoke bitterly. Martin shook his head.

"I have not seen them, except at a distance. Would a noble send a Christian to plead on his behalf? I can tell you they are thin from hunger. There is no one in the city who is not. There has been great suffering, Luke."

"If there has been suffering it was freely chosen. It does not take much to open a gate."

"If tyranny is waiting to come in, it does."

"Do you call me tyrant?"

"Whoever takes what a man will not freely give is that. A tyrant or a thief."

"You use harsh words, old friend," I said. "This thief, this tyrant, once saved you when you hung in chains, awaiting death by fire."

"Yes. For that, you may demand anything of me. But not of the city."

There was a sharpness in the air, almost of frost. Summer was giving way to autumn. Winter would follow soon.

I said: "The suffering is almost at an end. I do not need a gate to be opened now. Before the day is over my soldiers will walk through the shattered wall into the streets of Winchester. Or will your stable-god who worked such miracles work one here?"

"It may be. Through the weak bodies of his servants."

I laughed. "The Christians will build the wall again? I do not think they can build as fast as my mortar breaks it down."

Martin took off his spectacles and wiped his eyes. I saw that his hand trembled.

"You are not a cruel man, Luke," he said. "Only

blind. If you could see them starving, all those you knew—men and women, dwarf and human and polymuf—you would have pity. No, do not say it. They have only to open a gate. They can get bread in exchange for freedom. And meanwhile they are behind walls and you do not see them. But we will make you see."

"You waste your time," I said. "It is almost over. And I have won."

"Not yet." He pushed the spectacles back onto his nose. "I said the truth I have found gives a meaning to life. To death, also. I will leave you now. When I return to the city I will stand in the breach of the wall. I fear the thought as much as any man would, maybe more than most, but I think God will give me strength. Your bombs will shatter flesh and bone as well as stone." He smiled. "You have reminded me that I owe you a death. I am glad to repay it in this fashion."

"You speak bravely," I said, "and I believe that you would do it, with or without the help of your god. But I win here also. I have guards within call. You will not go back to the city until I am master of it."

"Imprison me if you wish," Martin said. "It makes no difference. I was sent here because I was your friend. There are others who will do this task, many others. The High Seers have brought you field glasses, I see, as well as a mortar. Use them to look at the wall."

The light was feeble still. With the naked eye one saw only the wall's gray shape, with the ragged V where the mortar bombs had crumbled it. But the glasses showed me other things. Small figures stood in the embrasure or clung to the broken edges of the wall. I counted a score of them, and more. I thought I saw the bald head of the Bishop. I remembered his words in Blodwen's apartment:

"If killing there must be I would rather it were done by a warrior who kills with his own hand, and knows what bloody corpse he leaves behind."

While I watched they began singing. One of their dirge-like hymns; it sifted thinly down through the cold dawn air.

"Give the order to fire whenever you choose," Martin said. "But this time you will not be blind. This time you will see what it is you do."

• • •

Men came from their tents, attracted by the singing. Cymru and Snake and Kluellan came to me, and the High Seers. They watched the singing Christians in the breach, and watched me also. Other figures appeared on top of the walls. They lined the parapets, in scores, in hundreds. There were not so many Christians in Winchester. These were the people of the city, human and dwarf and polymuf, offering their bodies as its bulwark.

I said to Martin: "Go back to them. Tell them they can keep their freedom."

TEN

THE SWORD OF THE SPIRITS

I N SLEEP LAST NIGHT I WAS IN WINCHESTER. I dreamed of an afternoon when Edmund and Martin and I climbed Catherine's Hill together, with the sun burning out of blue gulfs of sky and the clouds huge and white and slow-sailing. We had taken nets with us to catch butterflies, but all we saw were cabbage whites which were not worth taking. So we lay on the grass, under the shade of the trees which cover the hilltop, and talked idly as boys will talk on hot summer days: of dreams and hopes and nonsense. And when it was time to go home for tea we started down the hill, and Edmund cried: "Race you to the bottom!" and we began to run. Edmund and I left Martin behind and Edmund began to outdistance me also. So I ran faster and faster, taking giant strides, and then as the descent grew steeper I was skipping over the grass, unable to stop or check myself, until my feet left the ground altogether and I cartwheeled through the air, and the whole earth seemed to rise up and crash against me.

All this was as it happened. I remembered lying on the ground, dazed, my head throbbing savagely with pain, and Edmund and Martin coming to pick me up. I remembered the concern in their faces and even the shirt Edmund was wearing, blue with a patch at the elbow.

But there the dream changed. I was in bed and smarting from different wounds—the burns I got in my struggle with the Bayemot. And Blodwen stood by me, in her dress that was the color of beech leaves in winter. She took my bandaged hand and said: "You are a fool, Luke. But very brave . . ." She said: "There is to be a banquet where my father will give you a great honor. A prize. Do you want to know what prize it is, brave, foolish Luke?" She leaned forward, laughing, her golden hair falling almost to touch my face. "A prize . . . ," she whispered.

My heart was open and easy. In my dream I said what I had never been able to say in life:

"I love you, Blodwen."

As I spoke the words she drifted from me. I called after her and she smiled and shook her head. I tried to rise and follow, but could not. Her figure faded in the distance, and I awoke and found my pillow wet with tears, and the high towers of Klan Gothlen framed in the window opposite my bed.

It is three years since I led the army of the Wilsh back across the Burning Lands. Cymru calls me his son. He governs in name but leaves the exercise of authority to me. I am to be Cymru after him, and the people applaud this. Although a foreigner, I am their hero. The great painting of Luke and the Bayemot covers one wall of the throne room, and Gwulum and his apprentice artists have nearly finished the other one that faces it. It is called "The Conquest of the South" and shows me at Cymru's side in the Battle of the Itchen. My sword is raised to strike down a Captain who menaces him.

The High Seers came with us to Klan Gothlen.

They do not call themselves High Seers any longer and do not practice mumbo jumbo and give messages from the Spirits in darkened halls. They are scientists. They have set up schools and a university, at which the ancient knowledge is freely taught.

The Wilsh take gladly to this learning. Almost every day, it seems, there are new machines and devices to change our way of life. Last week a motor car chugged uneasily along the main street of the city, to the cheers of the onlookers. There is talk of building a railway to make easier our conquest and development of the savage lands. As soon as the engineers can make up their minds as to whether it will be twin-rail or monorail, the project will be put underway.

My people are happy and contented. Snake is a good Chancellor and Kluellan keeps the army at a high pitch of ceremonial drill: there is no real need for anything else. Hans is busily occupied with this notion of a railway. He has married a girl of human stock, though not much taller than he is, and they have a human child, a daughter.

Our local Christians still sing well, and their numbers still dwindle. The Bishop, who comes often

to the palace and whom I have learned to tolerate—
he has a sharp wit after all—is enthusiastic for
Science. He has even written a book, extolling its
spiritual values.

Our writ runs, with increasing sureness, to the
edge of the Burning Lands. We have no contact with
the parts beyond. Not long after our return a small
eruption sealed the pass. This is a temporary
thing—the scientists say the volcanoes are dying
down—but it has cut us off from the south.

I am glad of it, though the isolation cannot last.
Even if the pass stays closed there are other ways of
meeting. There is a town being built by the sea at the
mouth of the River Mawddach, under the shadow of
Cader Idris, and ships big enough to be safe from
any Bayemot will go out from there. In a few years
we shall have flying machines as well. The Burning
Lands will offer no barrier.

So we shall meet with the cities of the south
again, and when we do we shall conquer them. It will
not serve them to line their walls with the living
bodies of their citizens. We shall have weapons more
subtle and more powerful than Sten guns and mor-
tars: weapons of ease and novelty and riches. We

shall conquer them because we represent the strength of the future, and they the past which must always bow to it. It will happen because it must, but I am in no great hurry to see it.

I am content here much of the time. I busy myself with work and government. It is the hours of idleness that chafe. Cymru would have me marry and the Wilsh nobles tempt me with their daughters. They are pretty enough, some of them beautiful, but they do not move me.

The Sword of the Spirits lies in a golden casket in the throne room. Swords have no use any longer, though there was a fashion last winter of wearing ornamental daggers, but this one is treasured for its history and will be as long as the towers of Klan Gothlen stand and Cymru rules there. It is a trophy, a legacy, that a man would be glad to leave to his son.

But I shall have no son.

Turn the page for a peek at another
adventure series by John Christopher.

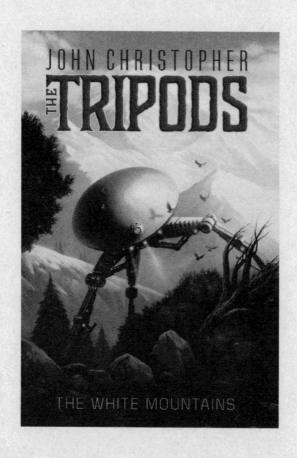

APART FROM THE ONE IN THE CHURCH TOWER, there were five clocks in the village that kept reasonable time, and my father owned one of them. It stood on the mantelpiece in the parlor, and every night before he went to bed he took the key from a vase, and wound it up. Once a year the clockman came from Winchester, on an old jogging packhorse, to clean and oil it and put it right. Afterward he would drink camomile tea with my mother, and tell her the news of the city and what he had learned in the villages through which he had passed. My father, if he were not busy milling, would stalk out at this time, with some contemptuous remark about gossip; but later, in the evening, I would hear my mother passing the stories on to him. He did not show much enthusiasm, but he listened to them.

My father's great treasure, though, was not the clock, but the Watch. This, a miniature clock with a dial less than an inch across and a circlet permitting it to be worn on the wrist, was kept in a locked drawer of his desk; and only brought out to be worn on ceremonial occasions, like Harvest Festival, or a Capping. The clockman was only allowed to see to it every third year, and at such times my father stood by, watching him as he worked. There was no other Watch in the village, nor in any of the villages round about. The clockman said there were a number in Winchester, but none as fine as this. I wondered if he said it to please my father, who certainly showed pleasure in the hearing, but I believe it truly was of very good workmanship. The body of the Watch was of a steel much superior to anything they could make at the forge in Alton, and the works inside were a wonder of intricacy and skill. On the front was printed "Anti-magnetique Incabloc," which we supposed must have been the name of the craftsman who made it in olden times.

The clockman had visited us the week before, and I had been permitted to look on for a time while he cleaned and oiled the Watch. The sight fascinated me, and after he had gone I found my thoughts running continually on this treasure, now locked away again in its drawer. I was, of course, forbidden to touch my father's desk and the notion of opening a locked drawer in it should have been unthinkable. Nonetheless, the idea persisted. And after a day or two, I admitted to myself that it was only the fear of being caught that prevented me.

On Saturday morning, I found myself alone in the house. My father was in the mill room, grinding, and the servants—even Molly who normally did not leave the house during the day—had been brought in to help. My mother was out visiting old Mrs. Ash, who was sick, and would be gone an hour at least. I had finished my homework, and there was nothing to stop my going out into the bright May morning and finding Jack. But what completely filled my mind was the thought that I had this opportunity to look at the Watch, with small chance of detection.

The key, I had observed, was kept with the other keys in a small box beside my father's bed. There were four, and the third one opened the drawer. I took out the Watch, and gazed at it. It was not going, but I knew one wound it and set the hands by means of the small knob at one side. If I were to wind it only a couple of turns it would run down quite soon—just in case my father decided to look at it later in the day. I did this, and listened to its quiet rhythmic ticking. Then I set the hands by the clock. After that it only remained for me to slip it on my wrist. Even notched to the first hole, the leather strap was loose; but I was wearing the Watch.

Having achieved what I had thought was an ultimate ambition, I found, as I think is often the case, that there remained something more. To wear it was a triumph, but to be seen wearing it . . . I had told my cousin, Jack Leeper, that I would meet him that morning, in the old ruins at the end of the village. Jack, who was nearly a year older than myself and due to be presented at the next Capping, was the person, next to my parents, that I most admired. To take the Watch out of the house was to add enormity to disobedience, but having already gone so far, it was easier to contemplate it. My mind made up, I was determined to waste none of the precious time I had. I opened the front door, stuck the hand with the Watch deep into my trouser pocket, and ran off down the street.

The village lay at a crossroads, with the road in which our house stood running alongside the river (this giving power for the mill, of course) and the second road crossing it at the ford. Beside the ford stood a small wooden bridge for foot travelers, and I pelted across, noticing that the river was higher than usual from the spring rains. My Aunt Lucy was approaching the bridge as I left it at the far end. She called a greeting to me, and I called back, having first taken care to veer to the other side of the road. The baker's shop was there, with trays of buns and cakes set out, and it was reasonable that I should be heading that way: I had a couple of pennies in my pocket. But I ran on past it, and did not slacken to a walk until I had reached the point where the houses thinned out and at last ended.

The ruins were a hundred yards farther on. On

one side of the road lay Spiller's meadow, with cows grazing, but on my side there was a thorn hedge, and a potato field beyond. I passed a gap in the hedge, not looking in my concentration on what I was going to show Jack, and was startled a moment later by a shout from behind me. I recognized the voice as Henry Parker's.

Henry, like Jack, was a cousin of mine—my name is Will Parker—but, unlike Jack, no friend. (I had several cousins in the village: people did not usually travel far to marry.) He was a month younger than I, but taller and heavier, and we had hated each other as long as I could remember. When it came to fighting, as it very often did, I was outmatched physically, and had to rely on agility and quickness if I were not going to be beaten. From Jack I had learned some skill in wrestling which, in the past year, had enabled me to hold my own more, and in our last encounter I had thrown him heavily enough to wind him and leave him gasping for breath. But for wrestling one needed the use of both hands. I thrust my left hand deeper into the pocket and, not answering his call, ran on toward the ruins.

He was closer than I had thought, though, and he pounded after me, yelling threats. I put a spurt on, looked back to see how much of a lead I had, and found myself slipping on a patch of mud. (Cobbles were laid inside the village, but out here the road was in its usual poor condition, aggravated by the rains.) I fought desperately to keep my footing, but would not, until it was too late, bring out my other hand to help balance myself. As a result, I went slithering and sprawling and finally fell. Before I could recover, Henry was kneeling across me, holding the back of my head with his hand and pushing my face down into the mud.

This activity would normally have kept him happy for some time, but he found something of greater interest. I had instinctively used both hands to protect myself as I fell, and he saw the Watch on my wrist. In a moment he had wrenched it off, and stood up to examine it. I scrambled to my feet, and made a grab, but he held it easily above his head and out of my reach.

I said, panting, "Give that back!"

"It's not yours," he said. "It's your father's."

I was in agony in case the Watch had been dam-
aged, broken maybe, in my fall, but even so I
attempted to get my leg between his, to drop him.
He parried, and, stepping back, said,

"Keep your distance." He braced himself, as
though preparing to throw a stone. "Or I'll see how
far I can fling it."

"If you do," I said, "you'll get a whipping for it."

There was a grin on his fleshy face. "So will you.
And your father lays on heavier than mine does. I'll
tell you what: I'll borrow it for a while. Maybe I'll let
you have it back this afternoon. Or tomorrow."

"Someone will see you with it."

He grinned again. "I'll risk that."

I made a grab at him. I had decided that he was
bluffing about throwing it away. I almost got him
off balance, but not quite. We swayed and struggled,
and then crashed together and rolled down into the
ditch by the side of the road. There was some water
in it, but we went on fighting, even after a voice
challenged us from above. Jack—for it was he who
had called to us to get up—had to come down and
pull us apart by force. This was not difficult for

him. He was as big as Henry, and tremendously strong also. He dragged us back up to the road, got to the root of the matter, took the Watch off Henry, and dismissed him with a clip across the back of the neck.

I said tearfully, "Is it all right?"

"I think so." He examined it, and handed it to me. "But you were a fool to bring it out."

"I wanted to show it to you."

"Not worth it," he said briefly. "Anyway, we'd better see about getting it back. I'll lend a hand."

Jack had always been around to lend a hand, as long as I could remember. It was strange, I thought, as we walked toward the village, that in just over a week's time I would be on my own. The Capping would have taken place, and Jack would be a boy no longer.

Jack stood guard while I put the Watch back and returned the drawer key to the place where I had found it. I changed my wet and dirty trousers and shirt, and we retraced our steps to the ruins. No one knew what these buildings had once been, and I think one of the things that attracted us was a sign, printed on a chipped and rusted metal plate:

DANGER

6,600 VOLTS

We had no idea what Volts had been, but the notion of danger, however far away and long ago, was exciting. There was more lettering, but for the most part the rust had destroyed it. LECT CITY: we wondered if that were the city it had come from.

Farther along was the den Jack had made. One approached it through a crumbling arch; inside it was dry, and there was a place to build a fire. Jack had made one before coming out to look for me, and had skinned, cleaned, and skewered a rabbit ready for us to grill. There would be food in plenty at home—the midday meal on a Saturday was always lavish—but this did not prevent my looking forward greedily to roast rabbit with potatoes baked in the embers of the fire. Nor would it stop me doing justice to the steak pie my mother had in the oven. Although on the small side, I had a good appetite.

We watched and smelled the rabbit cooking in companionable silence. We could get on very well together without much conversation, though normally I had a ready tongue. Too ready, perhaps—I knew that a lot of the trouble with Henry arose because I could not avoid trying to get a rise out of him whenever possible.

Jack was not much of a talker under any circumstances, but to my surprise, after a time he broke the silence. His talk was inconsequential at first, chatter about events that had taken place in the village, but I had the feeling that he was trying to get around to something else, something more important. Then he stopped, stared in silence for a second or two at the crisping carcass, and said,

"This place will be yours, after the Capping."

It was difficult to know what to say. I suppose if I had thought about it at all, I would have expected that he would pass the den on to me, but I had not thought about it. One did not think much about things connected with the Cappings, and certainly did not talk about them. For Jack, of all people, to do so was surprising, but what he said next was more surprising still.

"In a way," he said, "I almost hope it doesn't work. I'm not sure I wouldn't rather be a Vagrant."

I should say something about the Vagrants. Every village generally had a few—at that time there were four in ours, as far as I knew—but the number was constantly changing as some moved off and others took their place. They occasionally did a little work, but whether they did or not the village supported them. They lived in the Vagrant House, which in our case stood on the corner where the two roads crossed and was larger than all but a handful of houses (my father's being one). It could easily have accommodated a dozen Vagrants, and there had been times when there had been almost that many there. Food was supplied to them—it was not luxurious, but adequate—and a servant looked after the place. Other servants were sent to lend a hand when the House filled up.

What was known, though not discussed, was that the Vagrants were people for whom the Capping had proved a failure. They had Caps, as normal people did, but they were not working properly. If this were going to happen, it usually showed itself in the first day or two following a Capping: the person who had been Capped showed distress, which increased as the days went by, turning at last into a fever of the brain. In this state, they were clearly in much pain. Fortunately the crisis did not last long; fortunately also, it happened only rarely. The great majority of Cappings were entirely successful. I suppose only about one in twenty produced a Vagrant.

When he was well again, the Vagrant would start his wanderings. He, or she; because it happened occasionally with girls, although much more rarely. Whether it was because they saw themselves as being outside the community of normal people, or because the fever had left a permanent restlessness in them, I did not know. But off they would go and wander through the land, stopping a day here, as long as a month there, but always moving on. Their minds, certainly, had been affected. None of them could settle to a train of thought for long, and many had visions, and did strange things.

They were taken for granted, and looked after, but, like the Cappings, not much talked about. Children, generally, viewed them with suspicion and avoided them. They, for their part, mostly seemed melancholy, and did not talk much, even to each other. It was a great shock to hear Jack say he half wished to be a Vagrant, and I did not know how to answer him. But he did not seem to need a response. He said, "The Watch—do you ever think what it must have been like in the days when things like that were made?"

I had, from time to time, but it was another subject on which speculation was not encouraged, and Jack had never talked in this way before. I said, "Before the Tripods?"

"Yes."

"Well, we know it was the Black Age. There were too many people, and not enough food, so that people starved, and fought each other, and there were all kinds of sicknesses, and . . ."

"And things like the Watch were made—by men, not the Tripods."

"We don't know that."

"Do you remember," he asked, "four years ago, when I went to stay with my Aunt Matilda?"

I remembered. She was his aunt, not mine, even

though we were cousins: she had married a foreigner. Jack said, "She lives at Bishopstoke, on the other side of Winchester. I went out one day, walking, and I came to the sea. There were the ruins of a city that must have been twenty times as big as Winchester."

I knew of the ruined great-cities of the ancients, of course. But these, too, were little talked of, and then with disapproval and a shade of dread. No one would dream of going near them. It was disquieting even to think of looking at one, as Jack had done. I said, "Those were the cities where all the murdering and sickness were."

"So we are told. But I saw something there. It was the hulk of a ship, rusting away so that in places you could see right through it. And it was bigger than the village. Much bigger."

I fell silent. I was trying to imagine it, to see it in my mind as he had seen it in reality. But my mind could not accept it.

Jack said, "And that was built by men. Before the Tripods came."

Again I was at a loss for words. In the end, I said lamely, "People are happy now."

Jack turned the rabbit on the spit. After a while, he said, "Yes. I suppose you're right."

The weather stayed fine until Capping Day. From morning till night people worked in the fields, cutting the grass for hay. There had been so much rain earlier that it stood high and luxuriant, a promise of good winter fodder. The Day itself, of course, was a holiday. After breakfast, we went to church, and the parson preached on the rights and duties of manhood, into which Jack was to enter. Not of womanhood, because there was no girl to be Capped. Jack, in fact, stood alone, dressed in the white tunic which was prescribed. I looked at him, wondering how he was feeling, but whatever his emotions were, he did not show them.

Not even when, the service over, we stood out in the street in front of the church, waiting for the Tripod. The bells were ringing the Capping Peal, but apart from that all was quiet. No one talked or whispered or smiled. It was, we knew, a great experience for everyone who had been Capped. Even the Vagrants came and stood in the same rapt silence.

But for us children, the time lagged desperately. And for Jack, apart from everyone, in the middle of the street? I felt for the first time a shiver of fear, in the realization that at the next Capping I would be standing there. I would not be alone, of course, because Henry was to be presented with me. There was not much consolation in that thought.

At last we heard, above the clang of bells, the deep staccato booming in the distance, and there was a kind of sigh from everyone. The booming came nearer and then, suddenly, we could see it over the roofs of the houses to the south: the great hemisphere of gleaming metal rocking through the air above the three articulated legs, several times as high as the church. Its shadow came before it, and fell on us when it halted, two of its legs astride the river and the mill. We waited, and I was shivering in earnest now, unable to halt the tremors that ran through my body.

Sir Geoffrey, the Lord of our Manor, stepped forward and made a small stiff bow in the direction of the Tripod; he was an old man, and could not bend much nor easily. And so one of the enormous burnished tentacles came down, gently and precisely, and its tip curled about Jack's waist, and it lifted him up, up, to where a hole opened like a mouth in the hemisphere, and swallowed him.

In the afternoon there were games, and people moved about the village, visiting, laughing, and talking, and the young men and women who were unmarried strolled together in the fields. Then, in the evening, there was the Feast, with tables set up in the street since the weather held fair, and the smell of roast beef mixing with the smells of beer and cider and lemonade, and all kinds of cakes and puddings. Lamps were hung outside the houses; in the dusk they would be lit, and glow like yellow blossoms along the street. But before the Feast started, Jack was brought back to us.

There was the distant booming first, and the quietness and waiting, and the tread of the gigantic feet, shaking the earth. The Tripod halted as before, and the mouth opened in the side of the hemisphere, and then the tentacle swept down and carefully set Jack by the place which had been left for him at

Sir Geoffrey's right hand. I was a long way away, with the children at the far end, but I could see him clearly. He looked pale, but otherwise his face did not seem any different. The difference was in his white shaved head, on which the darker metal tracery of the Cap stood out like a spider's web. His hair would soon grow again, over and around the metal, and, with thick black hair such as he had, in a few months the Cap would be almost unnoticeable. But it would be there all the same, a part of him now till the day he died.

This, though, was the moment of rejoicing and making merry. He was a man, and tomorrow would do a man's work and get a man's pay. They cut the choicest fillet of beef and brought it to him, with a frothing tankard of ale, and Sir Geoffrey toasted his health and fortune. I forgot my earlier fears, and envied him, and thought how next year I would be there, a man myself.

I did not see Jack the next day, but the day after that we met when, having finished my homework, I was on my way to the den. He was with four or five other men, coming back from the fields. I called him, and he smiled and, after a moment's hesitation, let the others go on. We stood facing each other, only a few yards from the place where, little more than a week earlier, he had separated Henry and me. But things were very different.

I said, "How are you?"

It was not just a polite question. By now, if the Capping were going to fail, he would be feeling the pains and discomfort that would lead, in due course, to his becoming a Vagrant. He said, "I'm fine, Will."

I hesitated, and blurted out, "What was it like?"

He shook his head. "You know it's not permitted to talk about that. But I can promise you that you won't be hurt."

I said, "But why?"

"Why what?"

"Why should the Tripods take people away, and Cap them? What right have they?"

"They do it for our good."

"But I don't see why it has to happen. I'd sooner stay as I am."

He smiled. "You can't understand now, but you

will understand when it happens. It's . . ." He shook his head. "I can't describe it."

"Jack," I said, "I've been thinking." He waited, without much interest. "Of what you said—about the wonderful things that men made, before the Tripods."

"That was nonsense," he said, and turned and walked on to the village. I watched him for a time and then, feeling very much alone, made my way to the den.